T006404

Desert Teacher

Desert Teacher

A collection of short stories

Arjun Singh

PARTRIDGE
A Penguin Random House Company

Because of the dynamic nature of the Internet, any web addresses or links contained in this book may have changed since publication and may no longer be valid. The views expressed in this work are solely those of the author and do not necessarily reflect the views of the publisher, and the publisher hereby disclaims any responsibility for them.

Print information available on the last page.

To order additional copies of this book, contact
Partridge India
000 800 10062 62
orders.india@partridgepublishing.com

www.partridgepublishing.com/india

For 24

Contents

Stop Thinking

"**S**top thinking," the doctor advised me.

"But Doctor, sir—" I replied.

"You think too much," he spoke again and wrote some prescriptions for medicines on the back of the same paper he used last time when I visited him a couple of weeks ago.

"How can I stop thinking? I am not dead," I asked.

He got annoyed this time. He examined the investigation reports and said, "*Bahut sochate ho* (you think too much). There is not any serious problem. Take the medicines and come back after a couple of weeks; it is just because you think too much. Next." He rang the bell, and the next patient waiting in the long queue came in. I came out of the doctor's room, went to the chemist's shop, and bought the prescribed medicines.

"One medicine is not available, so we can give you a substitute," the chemist suggested. Well, I did not want to take any medicine without the doctor's prescription, but to see him again to ask him about the substitute meant waiting again in a long queue. I was tired. I had travelled six hours in a crowded bus that morning, and I had to travel again to go back to Jaisalmer. I took all the medicine with the substitute one and went to the bus station.

I had been regularly visiting this doctor for the last three months; he was a popular neurosurgeon in Jodhpur. He said, "Nothing is serious," but I knew it was something very serious. I had regular headaches; I could not sleep very well at night. Although my body was sleeping, my brain was always busy. I had no rest at all—as a result, I was very tired in the day and did not like to talk to anyone about it. The problem was in class when I taught my students. After first period in the school, I felt that I had been teaching continuously for the last ten hours. I was noticing some changes in my behavior. I was getting aggressive with my students. Of course, there was something wrong with me.

My mother went to the temple and brought back holy water in a brass urn and threw it on me; my grandpa asked a priest to perform special devotions in the temple for my health, and he paid the fees. My father, carrying my horoscope, visited the astrologers in the city and finally bought a gold ring, jeweled in topaz; perhaps he took a loan to arrange that. My grandma took four lemons, touched them to my body four times, and went out into the street at midnight to throw them in all four directions. She also called a man who was a practitioner of black magic. A very old man wearing black clothes and carrying a bunch of peacock feathers ordered me to sit in front of him. I did not listen to him, but my grandma believed in ghosts and spirits and asked the black magician again.

"He is under the spell of a witch," he declared.

I smiled.

"He urinated on a grave," he roared this time and stared at me. "I give you seven days; it is my last warning. Leave him, or I will fix you in this dirty bottle and burn you with this hot iron rod." He showed the bottle and iron rod to me.

I looked back at my grandma. She was shivering with fear, praying with her hands folded.

The back magician whispered and closed his eyes awhile. "It is a very dangerous witch, but do not worry; I will control her." The black magician charged extra for his home visit and went to meet another patient to warn him with the same dirty bottle and iron rod.

"Come on, Grandma; your Arjun is just sick and will be better. Do not worry," I said to her.

"No, it is really a witch who is torturing you," my mother added.

"That is good; someone fell in love with your son." I winked.

"Stop this nonsense," my mother cried.

"You, too, Mom," I whispered. "Did you open my book safe?" I asked both ladies.

"No," my mother replied. "What is there in the safe? Only your books?"

"Then how do you know so much about witches and ghosts if you did not read Macbeth?" I asked just for fun. Both ladies failed to understand what I said. My mother and grandma never went to school and had great faith in the spirit world.

It was New Year's, midnight. People were watching television. Music was being played in a nearby restaurant.

"What is it today?" my mother asked me. I was very sick and sleeping on the bed; my head was in her lap, and she was massaging it with her thin fingers. I liked it.

I was feeling unwell, but I replied, "It is New Year's today. You know, people celebrate it just like *Deepavali*." She nodded, but I knew it was not easy for her to understand about the celebration of a very normal day, as she had no idea about the English calendar.

"Eat something," she pleaded. "I made potatoes; you know you like potatoes."

"No, Mom. I do not want to eat anything."

But she went into the kitchen and served the food. I tried to eat. I ate one chapati. I was not hungry, but I ate because she wanted me to eat.

"I am fine now; you go and sleep."

"No. I will sleep here," she said, and she slept on the floor. She was really very worried. Perhaps mothers know well when their kids are not happy.

I took pills and tried to sleep, but I felt like vomiting. I went to the bathroom and vomited. I could hear the firecrackers; people were celebrating the New Year. I came back into the room but vomited again and this time, on the bed. My mom woke up and called my brother and father, who were sleeping in the other room. I was shivering; I asked my brother to go for a taxi and said I wanted to go to a hospital. It was not easy for me to breathe now. I was feeling strangulated. My brother rushed for a taxi. My mother and father sat near me, massaging my back and shoulders. My grandfather came in and put his hand on me.

"Oh mighty God, save him," he prayed. My brother called our neighbor, who was a taxi driver. They took me to the hospital.

"I do not want to die," I cried. That was the last thing I remembered.

It was the next day, in the evening. I slowly opened my eyes. I was in the hospital; all my family members were standing near my bed.

"Thank God," my father said to my mother, who was sitting in the corner of the room waiting for me to open my eyes. "He is conscious now. How are you?" he asked me.

"I am fine," I replied.

The doctor came, checked my pulse, opened my eyes wide, used his stethoscope, and asked me to breathe, breathe, and breathe.

"He is out of danger now," he declared. It was a big relief for all of my family members; perhaps they had lost hope when I was admitted here last night. I closed my eyes and thanked Him

The next morning I felt better, took a glass of juice, and gave proper answers to all the questions the doctor asked me.

"Do you speak English at home?" he asked.

I smiled and said, "No, I speak *Jaisalmeri* (the local dialect)."

"You remember last night you were speaking in English?" he informed me.

"I do not remember," I replied. "I apologize if I spoke wrong or misbehaved."

"Do not worry; you were not in control," the doctor replied with love. "But you spoke well for sure," he smiled.

Perhaps he was a bit impressed with his new patient. "I like the soliloquy of Hamlet, 'to be or not to be.'" He was appreciative. "You spoke fluently."

"What else?" I asked.

"I am not a man of literature," he replied. "But I heard you asking some questions like, 'What am I to do? Where am I to go?' Some questions like this."

Oh my God, it means I was acting as Hamlet, the heroic character of Shakespeare's great tragedy, or acting as Eliza, heroine of Bernard Shaw's play Pygmalion.

I was not sure why I acted abnormally last night. What was in me? Who was speaking Hamlet's soliloquy and Eliza's questions? Was the magician correct? Was it a witch? No, it was not a witch; it was me, Arjun, who had suppressed his personality, killed his desires, failed to make a balance between what he learned at college and what he had been taught by his people, his society.

I was fighting against the Arjun whom I left years before when I left Jodhpur. He came back to me when I returned to Jaisalmer after my postgraduate course in English. I had new ideas and new thoughts. In those years I had travelled a lot; I had gone very far, but when I came back into my old world, I failed to make a balance.

I was working as a primary teacher in a remote village. People here were very traditional and had very deep-rooted and dogmatic beliefs. It was as if I had come into another age.

Nobody was interested in talking about the new world that was changing so fast. No one there believed that man had reached the moon. They did not want to change their rigidly held opinions; perhaps they felt wounded or threatened if someone argued with their beliefs. My fellow teacher, who was only qualified to teach higher secondary level, was now equal to me. We both had the same salary and the same treatment. I was so frustrated one day when I asked him to use a calculator. To my surprise, my fellow teacher left it aside and counted using his fingers. People did not want to adapt to anything new. I stayed there for two years, felt lonely, tried my best to adjust, and worked hard to get a better job as an English teacher in any of the secondary or higher schools of the district. Most of the posts for English teachers in these schools were always vacant, and the students always presented themselves for the exams without having had a teacher. But the reservation system whereby posts are reserved according the caste system always pushed me back.

One day I was teaching the fifth class. I took a piece of chalk and wrote some simple sentences on the blackboard. I asked the class to copy them. I sat in a chair and closed my eyes awhile. I heard my students talking with each other.

I opened my eyes and asked one of the students, "Have you written them all?" He looked confused and pointed to the blackboard. There were only two sentences of the lesson followed by: "I fall upon the thorns of life! I bleed!"

I was alone with my modern ideas, and the whole village was on the other side with its own old ideas. I fought bravely for two years. One morning I woke up with my body temperature near 102. It was fever.

"There is no bus today," my student informed me. I went back to my room; I was feeling cold; I had a headache.

"It is malaria," I thought. I spent the night waking without medicines and anyone to attend me. The next day, with the help of my students, I reached the mud road. I could not walk, so one of my students rushed to his father and came back with a camel. I reached a nearby village on the camel, where I could catch a bus to go to the city.

I was feeling safe now. I went to the hospital, where I was confronted by a long queue, but it was no problem; I was in the habit of waiting—waiting in long queues for buses, waiting in long queues to submit forms in college, and waiting in long queues to pay for water and electricity. My turn came, and I sat on the stool in front of the doctor.

"I am suffering from malaria." I did not realize it, but it was an attack on the doctor's ego. He wanted to declare, "It is malaria," because he was the doctor, not me.

"How you can say that?" he asked.

"The symptoms say so," I replied.

He wrote down some prescriptions and gave me the piece of paper. "Go and buy these medicines, but confirm with the chemist whether these medicines are antimalarial or not." Perhaps he was playing with me now. He was not serious about my problem.

I took the medicines, but there was no improvement. I went back to the hospital to another doctor. I showed him the medicines I had taken, and he smiled and wrote some very high-dose medicines to be taken for five days. I took all the prescribed medicines, but there was no improvement at all. And at last I was admitted to hospital. I stayed in hospital for five days. The doctor prescribed some more medicines for fifteen days and advised me to rest.

"I have a headache," I complained to the doctor.

"It was brain fever; that's why you were confused when you were admitted here. It will take time to improve," he advised.

I waited and waited, but I had regular headaches. I was now back at the village but was not as well as I was before. It looked like I would lose the battle I had been fighting for the last two years. But I continued my hard work with my students. My physical weakness due to brain fever and the mental problems of not adjusting had mingled, and now I was in a critical condition. I was sick, and I had lost my self-confidence, the most powerful weapon I had.

I decided to go to a doctor at Jodhpur and consult him about this regular headache.

"Stop thinking" was the only answer from him.

I was educated. I had qualifications. I had questions about the system I was working for and about the society I was living in: "Where am I to go? What am I to do? What have you left me fit for?" I could not go back to the village to work as a farmer and accept all the ignorance, but on the other hand, the system was not ready to give me the chance I deserved. That was the thinking that I suffered from for more than five years. It was like a horrible disease, and at one stage I thought that I would die from depression.

But the Arjun who came back from Jodhpur was not ready to surrender so soon. My journey from darkness to light was not so easily discouraged, and I was not ready to lose my way to my destination.

One day the disease declared by the doctor at Jodhpur who said, "You think too much," solved the problem; a problem that could not be solved by the great neurosurgeon and the great black magician was now solved on its own.

The problem had its own solution within it. I thought positively, analyzed it, and reached the conclusion. How can I beat my isolation? How can I make a good balance between the Arjun living in Jaisalmer and the Arjun who came from Jodhpur? How can I stop Hamlet and Eliza constantly disturbing me? How can I stop thinking too much?

Now, for the first time, I spoke English at home. My family members were surprised at this new change. They did not listen to me, but I was firm, and I continued with it. I had no more friends; perhaps people did not agree with my revolutionary thoughts.

I saved some money from my little salary to buy good novels. Books proved to be my best friends. I went to historical monuments on Sundays and other holidays, met many tourists from all over the world, and talked a lot with them about almost all matters. What intellectual people they were, always curious to learn, and giving one the chance to speak and listen with great concentration. Some of the tourists became very friendly to me. I wrote them letters and replied to their messages. What a positive change in me. I was feeling much better. I was happy, I could sleep well, and now I was not thinking too much, for sure.

I was still working as a primary teacher in the small rural village, but now I was not isolated and not locked into these circumstances. I had my own world, very broad and filled with good people. I had friends from outside India. They gave me a new life, enriched me, and inspired me to do my best where I was. I was doing my best to promote primary education in the rural village. Now I enjoyed this. And best of all, I had no more headaches. Hamlet and

Eliza were now back in the pages of the great books. They did not disturb me anymore. I was sure this time that if I went out of my mind, I would not speak of them but surely about my great friends living so far from me. I thanked my friends who had brought me back to life. And I had stopped thinking, and of course, I was living and enjoying life. I was back to life.

The Last Desire

I was getting ready to go to my village school.

"Stay here till evening if you can," my grandfather said to me. He was very sad and failed to hide his sorrow; for the first time, I saw him with wet eyes. The strong man who struggled a lot never gave a sign of sorrow to his family members in his life. I had been at home for the last couple of days. I had come home to see my grandma who was very sick. She was lying in bed, attended by my mother and my widowed aunt. She was very weak and could hardly speak.

My grandparents came from a part of Hindustan which became part of Pakistan in 1947. India was divided, and mostly Hindus came here to India, and Muslims went to Pakistan. My grandfather, who belonged to a rich family, left his birthplace with his elderly parents, his nine-year-old wife, his five brothers, and two young sisters. He was about seventeen when he came here. They stayed in a village near Jaisalmer. They had lost everything and started their struggle as farmers in this part of the land where droughts are always frequent.

My grandma said once to me, "We spent half of our life gazing toward the clouds in the sky." My grandparents, who had the responsibility for young brothers and sisters, spent their lives in poverty. They worked hard and gave a good education to my father, and he became a teacher. They also supported me and my younger brother in continuing our studies.

I went into the room to see my grandma again. I kept my hand on her head. She slowly opened her eyes, looked at me, and the tears rolled down from her dry eyes.

I controlled myself. "I am going to the village school, Ma," I said.

She tried to speak and said slowly, "I am fine. You go to your school but come back when you hear about me. I want to go on the shoulders of my grandchildren on my last journey."

I was sure she was not fine. I went to my grandpa and said, "I am not going."

Just that same day in the afternoon, my mother came to us, covering her face. She always covered her face when my grandpa was there. My grandparents and my parents lived in a joint family in one small house, but my grandpa never knew what my mother looked like. It was symbol of respect to cover the face in front of the parents of one's husband in our society; it was a symbol of respect toward one's elders, and so my mother, always out of respect for her elders, never showed her face to my grandpa.

She gestured for me to come into the room. "Grandma wants to talk to you and your father," she said.

My father and I entered the room; she raised her hand slowly and asked my father to come close. My father went near her bed, and she talked to my papa. I never expected what she said to my papa.

I soon went closer to them. Grandma again repeated what she had said. I clearly heard what she said; I did not want to believe. She said, "I want to taste meat".

My grandma, named Gomati, was a very religious woman as her name indicated. Gomati is a holy river of India like Ganga, and of course, she was simple and religious like the holy river Gomati. I saw her going to Hindu temples regularly; she was always very kind. She never ate nonvegetarian food in her whole life. She never permitted my mother to cook nonvegetarian food at home. But on some special occasions, if nonvegetarian food was cooked, she always went out of the home and kept herself on a fast and never even touched the utensils used for cooking. She even drank water at a neighbor's home on that day. She was a very determined lady and always helped my grandpa to make many decisions at the critical times of their lives. She was born and married in the Rajput (warriors) community, where to drink and eat nonvegetarian food is allowed by religion. But she had different religious views.

I was shocked how a lady who maintained her religious faith for the whole of her life was going to break it in the last stage of her life.

"I want to taste meat," she said to my father. He did not believe it and asked her again.

"Yes, I want to taste meat before I die."

How impossible it is for a person to press personality and individual will against religious faith, I thought.

I rushed to the market and bought what she wished to eat. My mother, for the first time, was cooking meat for the lady who never allowed cooking it. I told grandma that the food was ready. She did not open her eyes but opened her mouth slowly. I poured a small teaspoon of gravy from the cooked meat. She gulped it quickly without tasting it. I waited, but this time she closed her mouth and gestured to me to remove the food. That was the last time that she ate something. She died peacefully the next morning. She left a question for me to think about for the whole of my life. Why did she wish to do an antireligious act at the end of her life (as she thought and believed the whole of her life that to eat nonvegetarian is an antireligious act)? I never got the answer to it.

All our relatives and friends came and expressed their condolences. My grandma was dressed and decorated like a newly married bride, with her small ornaments. My father, my uncle, my younger brother, and I carried her body on our shoulders toward the cremation ground, about three kilometers from our home. Our grandpa joined the procession barefooted to pay homage and show love for a lady who shared all the moments of joy and sorrow with him. We slowly placed her body on the funeral pyre.

Ladies are not allowed to join the funeral ceremony, so it was my duty to remove the ornaments from her body. I took off a very old, simple necklace called *Mangal Sutra*, the necklace worn on the day of her wedding, and her silver anklets. Her body was lying calmly; I looked at her face, very calm like a tired traveler who had walked the whole night and was resting now in peace. My grandfather came to see her face for the last time; perhaps he was saying it was not me who made you struggle your whole life but the circumstances. My father and my brother came close, looked at her for the last time, and then we covered her face. My father set fire to the funeral pyre, and within half an hour, we were sitting near a heap of ashes.

The next day my grandfather's younger brother and I went back to the cremation ground to collect the ashes. I was standing close to the place where she was cremated. I was always afraid to go to the cremation ground, as I heard lots of stories of ghosts and witches when I was a child. But this time I had no fear; I could feel her presence, and how I could be afraid of a kind lady who protected me all her life? I poured a glass of milk on the heap of ashes. My uncle asked me to collect bones from the heap. It was very cold in the morning, but my fingers could feel the warm ashes as I was collecting small bones from the heap.

"Collect from head to toe," directed my uncle who was supervising me, keeping his distance. I controlled my tears awhile and then allowed them to roll down over my cold cheeks. I collected handfuls of bones and put them in a bronze urn. We left the cremation ground and reached a temple on the edge of a man-made lake. It was a big temple with a vast courtyard and an underground water tank. It was quite windy, and I could hear the blowing wind. A big banyan tree was there, right in the middle of the courtyard. My uncle asked me to sit under the tree, and he went to call the priest, who was going to perform all the duties of the death ceremony. I was here to bid my grandmother's soul good-bye.

My uncle knocked at the door of the room in the corner of the courtyard. The loud voice of a song from a Bollywood movie could be heard. An old man opened the door, wearing a dirty, pale-white *dhoti* (a long loincloth worn by many Hindu men in India) and a coat. My uncle touched the man's feet. He had a radio in his hand; he moved the button to lower the volume. My uncle spoke to him, and he said to stay there awhile. He went back into the room and after a while came out with some utensils, a bunch of sticks, and a bottle of oil. He asked me to go to the tank and take a bath 108 times.

I looked him and said, "It is very cold," but he announced again, "I want you to be pure before you sit in front of me." I was going to say no, but my poor uncle asked me to obey the priest.

I did not want to hurt my uncle's feelings. I went to the water tank, filled a bucket, and invented a new idea of taking a bath 108 times in the cold weather. I poured 108 glasses on my body and came back soon to the priest and reported to him, "Yes, sir, I have done what you told me. Now I am pure." I sat under the tree. The ground was wet and muddy, and the priest sat on a wooden stool. I sat down. He asked me to set the fire. I was feeling cold, so quickly I set fire to the bunch of sticks. He arranged his pots, leaves, flowers, grains, and beads around the fire. He started to recite the mantras. I could listen to the mantras but could not understand the meaning. After every mantra he asked me the name of my grandma. I was surprised that he was reciting long mantras but forgetting the small name of my grandma. Perhaps he was more interested in listening to the song played on the radio. It took about an hour to complete the whole ceremony. Then he asked me to pay for this program. I asked my uncle and then started a shocking process of bargaining. The priest was demanding more because my father, who was supposed to perform the duties, was absent because of his sickness, and I acted in his place, so we had to pay a penalty.

I did not want to interrupt, but when I saw the priest cursing my uncle and my family, I went close to him and said, "Whatever we had, we have given to you."

He became very annoyed and declared, "Your grandma will go to hell if you will not pay what I told you."

I replied, "Let her go, then, if that's your decision."

He was now very angry. My uncle tried to calm him down and gave him the proper fees for his job and requested him not to curse.

The priest waited awhile. He thought and declared, "Tell the young boy to wash my legs and drink the same water." My uncle looked at me. Perhaps he wanted a positive reply from my side. But this time I was not going to follow either the priest or my poor uncle. If I did this, it was going to hurt the feelings of my whole family who contributed to my education. Perhaps both of them were waiting for me to say yes. I could do it, but education had changed the grandson of the kind and uneducated grandparents. I knew that if there is heaven and hell, then of course my grandparents deserved heaven, and the stupid priest definitely deserved the hell that he was threatening others with.

I came out without speaking a single word. My uncle followed me and never asked me why I disobeyed him and the priest. Perhaps he agreed with me but did not dare to revolt. I looked at him as he kept his hand on my shoulder and wanted to say something, but I could feel that he was going to say, "Bravo." Yes, a similar word in local dialect, *Shabash*, was what he said.

Cursed Question

I was trying to check my mail on the Internet. The speed was very slow, so I waited for half an hour, only to be disappointed—I could not get access. I left the Internet café. On the way back home, my cell phone rang; I checked it and saw unknown numbers twinkling on the display. I heard the very weak and sad voice of a lady.

"Arjun Bhaiya…?"

"Yes, that's me. I replied.

"Arjun Bhaiya, this is me, Geeta. My father-in-law is in very serious condition, and he is in the hospital. Please, would you and go and check how he is."

Geeta had never called me before by phone; in fact, this was the first time in sixteen years since we last spoke on the occasion of the death of my close friend, Om. I did not hesitate and rushed to the hospital. I found some of my neighbors there, wandering in the hospital corridors.

Raman, Om's brother, came out sighing, "He is no more."

Again my cell phone rang, and without waiting to hear any word from my side, Geeta asked nervously, "How is he?"

"He is no more," I replied.

Geeta had been Om's wife, and it was she whom I once thought I could help after Om's sad death. But I could not dare to help her or even talk to her, being prevented by invisible but very real social restrictions. I was in doubt that any help I might give would ruin her forever; this world of ours is full of such narrow-minded people.

Om…I miss him. I had few friends when I was in school. Suffice to say that perhaps it was my younger brother, in the same school as me, who was my best friend. My thin and weak body was always the reason for other students to make fun of me. But there was a boy who always helped me in my homework in mathematics, as I was very poor at this subject. Perhaps the reason I was so bad was because of the rather vindictive and horrible teacher and not the subject, the intricacies, or the logical questions of mathematics itself. I was always nervous and afraid in the mathematics periods because the teacher always asked the typical questions and never gave enough time to make any calculations; perhaps he was expecting the answers more quickly than any calculator. I never got to answer his questions on time or to his satisfaction and got many *chammats* (slaps) on my small, thin face.

What good news, then, for me when I did not see him in prayers one day. It meant no more beatings. Thank God he was on leave that day. How cruel he had been to me one day when I dared to appeal to him about what seemed to be an illogical and unjust marking given to a bullying classmate.

It was just after our half-yearly exam. We were sitting in the class and waiting for the teacher. He came with our answer sheets in hand. He sat and roared, "You are the dullest and most stupid boys I have ever seen in my life."

He gave answer sheets to all the students one by one. I got twenty-five out of a possible seventy. For me this was a good score, and I was very satisfied with the marks. But to my surprise, the boy sitting in the front row was waving the answer sheet proudly. He turned back slowly, smiled, and showed his answer sheet to us: "seventy-two out of seventy" was marked on the answer sheet with red ball pen. Surely a mistake, I thought, slip of the pen for sure. The boy who got more than maximum marks I knew was not so brilliant at mathematics as to exceed the maximum score—indeed, he was not so good to me either; he always pulled my bag or called me ugly names, and it was my turn, I thought, to complain to the teacher about him. I was thinking perhaps the teacher would punish him for not reporting the error. I went to him; he was making a list of the students. I wanted to appeal or rather make a request; well, you could not dare to ask a teacher a question, but it came out like one.

"Ajeet got more marks than the maximum marks—is this right?" He ignored me. So I asked again.

He looked at me with a fierce look and slapped me hard on my face. "Shut up. He works hard; if you work hard, you would get marks like him."

I was shocked, rushed back to my seat, and could not dare to look at my fellow students. I was so filled with shame, I wept bitterly that day. It was so unfair. That was the last question I ever asked any teacher in my student life.

I was not sure what mistake I had made. It seemed such an obvious error—why had he slapped me down? The next day we got our progress cards, and I asked my true friend Om to find out what were the real marks that Ajeet had got in mathematics and why he had been oddly given seventy-two out of seventy. Yes, said Om, it was an error on my teacher's side. Twenty-seven was written on the card. My proud teacher was not ready to admit that he made a mistake while writing the mark on Ajeet's paper itself. Perhaps the teachers were not supposed to make any mistakes, but what a pity they were not supposed to be seen to make mistakes and that they would not accept their mistakes. Om sympathized with the unfairness of my treatment. I had asked a cursed question.

I was also not good at playing games. It was Om who helped me in the classroom, and at playground he was a very good cricket player. I used to play with him in the street. His parents were from the same village where I belonged. His father was a peon in a government office. I remember the day when I was going to Jodhpur and Om came with me to the bus station to say good-bye. We had passed twelfth class, but he was not going to join the college. His father wanted him to work in a factory to support the extended family. Om really wanted to join college, but he was a very obedient son who sacrificed his career for his family.

I went to Jodhpur and did not meet Om for more than six months. Distance always changes a man. We promised to write each other, but both failed to keep the promise. I came to know he was very busy working hard in a factory and also worked part time to save money for his sister's marriage.

Being a good friend of Om's, I attended the entire program held at Om's home after his father's death. At the time it looked unbearable to me when a big feast was arranged on the twelfth day after the death of Om's father. I well understood the poor economic condition of Om's family, but it was not easy to interrupt the family matters of others. All the responsibility of paying for all the expenses fell on Geeta. I think she spent her few savings paying for the entire long program of twelve days and paying the priest, too.

She had passed eighth class when she got married. She wanted somehow to continue her studies, but her mother-in-law (Om's mother) asked her to perform all domestic work. The day she entered her in-laws' home, she performed all the housework with all her efficiency. Her mother-in-law was able to sit back and live on a complete rest routine now. Geeta was happy, but sometimes God makes the decision that is simply called His wish, but it destroys everything in someone's life. Om's death was very suspicious; he was in the hospital for more than a month. His father attended him personally, but Geeta was allowed only once to see him just for several minutes.

I remember the day well when she came to see Om in the hospital. She stayed near Om's bed for some minutes covering her face and wanted to ask Om something, but the presence of her in-laws stopped her from speaking. I could see the teardrops falling continuously on Om's palm. Om slowly closed his palm; perhaps he was trying to stop the time, but he failed. Just after a week, he breathed his last.

It was a terrible life for a widow that Geeta had been living since Om's death. She had two kids, and she forgot everything when she involved herself in looking after her in-laws and her kids. Time was going so fast for everyone but not for Geeta.

The following story tells of the cursed day for Geeta. It was a local festival, and all the neighbor ladies gathered in Om's house. A young lady was telling about a TV serial that was promoting the program of family planning. Geeta did not know that her knowledge was going to prove a curse for her life. She was telling the other ladies about the mission that was launched many years ago to check the population by sterilization. She told how the men were sterilized during that mission by force.

Just to prove the fact, she asked her mother-in-law a question. It was a blunder. She asked, "Babuji (her father-in-law) has also been operated on by this mission, has he not?" Her mother-in-law nodded, but destiny played its awful role with this question of Geeta's. Geeta asked and forgot, but her mother-in-law stored this question in her memory forever.

The next day Geeta faced a fierce look from her mother-in-law. She asked Geeta, "How do you know that my husband is also sterilized?"

Geeta trembled with fear and could feel the disaster. She answered very gently, "I read in a book about that mission, that most of the government employees were operated on, and I believe Babuji was a government employee, so he might have faced that operation." Geeta gave a true answer; Babuji was like her father—how could she think about this relation in any other way? But it was too late. Geeta's mother-in-law had made up her mind that there was an illegal relationship between Geeta and her husband. Bad news always travels fast.

She blamed Om's father, and that was the last time Babuji was seen smiling. Om's death and the blame of being corrupted robbed peace and happiness from the lives of both innocent persons.

I was at the cremation ground and could see the body of Om's father being cremated. Flames were rising high as if something had been suppressed somewhere for years and was now hurrying to be free in open sky, mingled with the grieved spirit of an innocent man. Was this the only answer to escape from lifelong suffering? Would Geeta have to wait for the same escape? I could not dare to help Geeta. I was not worried about myself; I had well-educated family members, but to deal with Geeta's mother-in-law was challenging. How could a woman be so unkind to another woman?

A month after Om's father's death, I asked my wife about Geeta. I never saw her leave home. I asked her to meet Geeta.

"She is like a stone," my wife told me when she came back from Geeta's home. "I talked to her, and she listened but did not speak. There were no gestures on her face, no tears in her dry eyes; her emotions have died."

"Did she tell you about her kids?" I asked.

"Yes. She said, 'I cannot change circumstances, but I will change the results this time.'" Geeta was looking very confident when she spoke about her kids. Geeta's sons were reading in secondary school and were very good at study. Perhaps Geeta was trying to make them brave enough to fight for themselves. She worked hard, sewed clothes, and earned some money for her children's education.

Widowed Aunt

This is the story of my aunt, widowed after eighteen years of marriage, and the even sadder story of why, in India, widows are ostracized by their society who believes they are bad luck.

"Are you the son of Mr. Laxman Singh?" the doctor asked me.

"No, he has no children. I am his wife's nephew," I replied.

"Then call someone who is a close relation," the doctor said.

I told the doctor all his relatives lived in Jaisalmer, but my aunt was here (in Jodhpur) if he wanted to talk to her.

The doctor thought awhile and said, "I am sorry to say both Mr. Singh's kidneys have failed, and it is better if you take him back home because there is no more chance."

I was shocked but with great courage asked the doctor again, what he meant by "no more chance." He said Mr.

Singh was in his last stage of life and had maybe four or five days more.

I came out of the doctor's chamber very sad and worried. I went to the general ward where my aunt was sitting near my uncle's bed. She had not slept for a couple of nights and was very tired. She asked me what the doctor told me. I had no words, so I said everything was fine.

When I came out of the hospital, I called my father and told him what the doctor told me. He was quiet for a while and then said, "Boy, take care of them till I reach Jodhpur."

My father arrived the next morning and met with the doctor, who told him there was nothing more to be done. But we told my aunt her husband was doing quite well and that we were going back to Jaisalmer. Tears rolled down her face; she understood this meant she was going to lose her beloved soon.

I still feel guilty about leaving my aunt there alone with my sick uncle. Despite many attempts, they had not been able to have children of their own, and so had treated my sister and me as their own.

A week later we received the news of my uncle's death. I met my aunt a few days later, and she embraced me and wept bitterly. For the next six months, she did not leave her house. When she did emerge, clad in black, as dictated by the customs of our society, we took her into our home.

What is the condition of the widows in our society? Widows suffer a very miserable life here. They are not allowed to remarry. They are not allowed to wear colorful clothes or jewelry. They are not allowed to attend weddings or festivals. They are not supposed to participate in certain ceremonies like tying the thread during *Raksha Bandhan*.

They are not even allowed to listen to music. If they step in the way of someone, it is a bad omen.

Why? The answer from our social system is the widow must be punished. Had the person not married this lady, he would have not died. It is believed the widow's bad luck takes a son from his parents and a father from his children. Like a compass needle that points north, man's accusing finger always finds a woman guilty in this male-dominated society.

My aunt suffered the life of a widow for a year. My family and I were very sad for her. Then we all made a challenging decision. We convinced her to find work somewhere. Finally, after many social objections, she joined a school as an attendant. She is very busy there with the children and has been ordered to wear colorful clothes by the school's administration. She passes her time well with the students and staff. She is happy now.

It took a lot for our family to go against the traditions of our society. And I think we were able to make that decision because we have been lucky enough to receive a good education. Truly an education can make change: it can change better than anything else.

Honeymoon

I got married in 1999. I had just completed my master's degree in English. My wife was studying philosophy in her final postgraduate year. It was an arranged marriage. We had never met or talked before our marriage. She was well educated, and that was very important for me.

When I first talked to her, it was just like an interview for any job. "Why did you select philosophy for your postgraduate course? What about your school life? What do you want to be? What is your hobby?"

I was not very interested or serious about the questions. What I wanted was for her to talk with me. She answered all the questions hesitantly, facing toward the wall. Something that attracted me was her answer about her hobby. To my surprise, she liked to watch Hollywood movies. It was quite strange. She was from a traditional family, and she was not allowed to talk to the person with whom she was going to spend the whole of her life, and here she was talking about Marilyn Monroe and Audrey Hepburn. I knew that in her parent's society, girls are not allowed to watch English-language movies. She dared to watch these movies. It was a good sign for me.

For two months we performed our duty as husband and wife. It was like beginning a new job: no feelings, no emotions, and no attachment.

I was worried about how an educated girl with modern values would adjust to my traditional family. Here she had to cover her face, was not allowed to talk to the elders, had to drop her studies, and put up with a lot of other social restrictions. Thank God both my family and she really adjusted to everything in a very intelligent way.

When she was out of my room, she was a perfect traditional lady, following all the traditional customs and in the evening arguing with me about democracy, ladies' rights, and other awful systems of society. We decided we would change things slowly. We planned how we would keep her studies continuing. And it's because of this understanding that she got a master's degree in political science, Hindi literature, and a teaching diploma after we got married. She got all her degrees through a correspondence course studying at home.

After two months I promised her that we would go for a honeymoon, but we always faced problems with money. It was a dream that took two long years to fulfill. By then, we had saved some money and decided to go to the hills north of Delhi. We had never been out of Rajasthan before. Permission from my family was more complicated than arranging the money. My grandmother said only one word: "nonsense."

My grandpa who loved me said, "Our home is the best place in the world for you to enjoy," paused, and after a long silence, said, "But be careful and come home soon." My father was flexible, supporting traditional values but at the same time feeling what he had missed following social traditions and customs. This time Papa was not forcing his opinions on his son, unlike when he was always forced to do what was decided by his parents. Papa said, "Well, I have no objection if Grandpa says yes. But do not say to everyone that you are going on your honeymoon but for your exams in Jodhpur."

I understood he could not dare to break the social traditions but simultaneously wanted his son to enjoy life as well. My mother happily said yes. I was surprised that as a big supporter of traditional values, she agreed so readily. We had hardly dared to ask her.

But later we came to know that our poor, innocent mother was impressed with a Hindi movie. In the film the newly married couple goes on their honeymoon and soon after their return, they have a baby.

She disclosed her secret when our son Girdhar was born five years after our marriage. My mother was happy and said that she had been waiting for this moment ever since we went on our honeymoon. But the opinions of the younger family members were interesting. Our brothers and sisters welcomed our daring decision. Perhaps they were thinking that we were going to make a way for them. Perhaps they hoped that they also would get the same chance to go and enjoy themselves when they got married. But none of them went; perhaps they heard about our bitter experiences on our journey.

We were very excited; we had never seen mountains, rivers, or flowers. In our home we had lots of photos of green landscapes with rivers, flowers, and snow. We were going to see and feel the beauty of nature.

We had no experience of a long journey. We took our luggage, thanked our parents, and went to the railway station for our journey to Delhi. There was a train for Delhi at four o'clock in the afternoon. We bought our tickets. It was third class ordinary compartment. The compartment was almost empty; about ten passengers were in the compartment. The journey by train was completely different from the journey by buses to the local villages in Jaisalmer. Lots of questions were asked by fellow passengers when we traveled by the village buses.

The most regular but striking question was, "Which caste do you belong to?" Once the same question was asked by an old passenger sitting next to me when I was traveling to the village where I teach.

I replied, "untouchables." I belong to an upper caste, but I wanted to know his opinions.

He started expressing his hate. "Bloody higher caste… treated us like animals.…"

I came to know how castes affect our lives here, even though it is said that the caste system is outdated.

We knew that our train would reach Delhi at ten o'clock in morning the next day. It was the month of June, and the temperature was about 115°F. It was very hot inside the iron compartment. Fortunately, fans were working. The train reached Jodhpur at eleven o'clock. We opened our dinner packet my mother had packed for us. Now the train was full with passengers. It was overcrowded, and it was not easy to move. If someone moved from his seat for the toilet, then he certainly did not get his seat back and had to travel the whole night standing in the corridor. It was a terrible night, staying awake the whole night and keeping an eye on our luggage. At ten o'clock in the morning, we arrived near Delhi. The train stopped, waiting for a signal. My wife was very tired. I asked her how she was, and she said, "fine," kneading her neck muscles, trying to ease her stiffness.

We saw slums everywhere out of the window. People were living so close to the railway track. Some were using the railway tracks as toilets in the open. It was stinking. The windows were framing awful, ugly scenes. It was not the place we came to see from so far. All the passengers were looking at each other with obvious doubts. No one could dare to offer a cup or glass to anyone. There were lots of stories of cheating or robbing fellow passengers by offering sweets, drinks, or fruits mixed in poison.

Suddenly this terrible peace was broken by the entry of a group of Hizras (eunuchs). They started to sing and dance. There was no platform in the compartment, so they were just moving their bodies ridiculously. They were making obscene gestures and using dirty language. This was the first time that we ever heard such use of our mother language, Hindi. After five minutes they stopped their horrible performances. They requested all the passengers to give them tips, but their request was more of a warning.

My wife, who was trying to keep her eyes away from them, looked at me and whispered for me to give some money quickly to them. I waited and found that all the passengers were giving some money; nobody made any objection. I gave them a fifty-rupee note.

Thank God, the train moved off slowly, and the Hijras made a quick move to get off the train. My wife was afraid, and so was I, but I tried to act normally. After an hour we reached the main station of Delhi. We found ourselves in an ocean of people. Everyone looked in a hurry. Pulling and pushing, we took our luggage and went into a corner. Some passengers avoided the main exit gate and took other ways to go out of the station, crossing the railway tracks. We understood these were passengers without tickets who wanted to get out of the station as soon as possible. We understood why some passengers were smiling when they saw tickets in my hand.

I kept the tickets out of my pocket to show them to the ticket collector, but no one was there to check the tickets. We had already decided to go to a budget hotel. At home on the History Channel, we once saw a program on Delhi, and we had an idea where we could find budget hotels. As we went out of the station, we faced the taxi drivers and the rickshaw men asking each and every passenger where to go. They looked so friendly, it seemed that they were our close relatives or friends whom we had known for years, but if they heard no, suddenly this appearance of affection quickly disappeared and was replaced by words of anger and hate, *Kangal* or *Makhichoos* (miser). Anyhow, we hired a rickshaw pulled by an old man. We felt guilty sitting while an old man, wet with sweat, was breathing hard, pulling us for a sum of money. We tried to control our emotions and looked here and there to avoid the miserable scene. A blast of diesel made us cough. Bloody pollution. This was no city for deep breathing. Beggars and poor people were on both sides of the streets. We had seen a lot of scenes like this on television, but for the first time, we experienced the stinking smell of the dirty polluted streets firsthand.

We reached the middle of a very busy street. Signboards of many hotels were hanging everywhere, saying, "Deluxe room," "Feel like home away from home," "Attached latrine & bath," and "TV in every room." We paid our rickshaw man and got out. Waste water was flowing down the middle of the street, and vegetable peelings, cigarette butts, eggshells, and plastic bags and bottles were bobbing along the surface. Planks had been thrown across to form walkways into the hotels and shops. We gingerly crossed the plank and went into one of the hotels.

We booked a room in a hotel that was very decorated on the outside and were shocked to find that it was more dirty and noisy inside. We paid in advance. But the man sitting at the reception did not continue looking as kind as he was trying to be before we paid. My wife had on traditional dress and was the center of attraction for all the people. And when we moved toward the room, the manager's eyes greedily followed her body. It made both of us uneasy.

We were tired, went into the room, and rested for some minutes. The room was not clean, plaster was falling off the walls, and it was filled with mosquitoes. The bed and pillow covers were different colors from their original because of the dirt. But at least we had an en-suite toilet. After resting for half an hour, I opened the door of the bathroom. To my surprise a large white bowl to sit on was fixed in one corner. I saw one like it once in a big sanitary shop in Jodhpur.

We were going to use it for the first time. I asked my wife, "Have you participated in gymnastics?"

She replied, "No, but why?"

"It's a big challenge for us to do a balancing act," I replied.

I positioned on it in local style. To balance, I took hold of the tap.

She chuckled. "You are a true Indian."

I smiled. "Yes."

Perhaps she got the idea from how I used the toilet. Perhaps I was a good example in accepting change, finely balancing the body two feet in the air.

We were very tired, so just after taking a bath, we decided to take a short rest before going out sightseeing. Suddenly I woke up. I heard someone running fast in the corridor. I quickly opened the door, but no one was there. I closed the door, and I noticed a small hole in one corner of the door. I understood the matter. After an hour someone knocked at the door. A thin boy of about twelve years old, holding a plastic jug of water, was at the door. He offered me the jug. I called him into the room and asked his name.

"Arjun," he replied.

I said, "It's me." He said his name was also Arjun.

I told him that I was a teacher in a primary school, and the students in my school were of his age. I asked about his family and his village. The soft-spoken words made the boy comfortable, and he became friendly.

He said, "Sir, this hotel is not good for the family. In the evening bad people come here."

I understood the situation quickly. There are hotels everywhere in India, mostly in the metropolitan and touristy cities. Delhi, the capital of India, is one of the most important cities of India; it has its own charm. It is like a magnet that draws all kinds of people, rich, middle class, and poor. Thousands of jobless young persons from all over India take the train to Delhi or arrive at the bus station every day in search of jobs. It is in the center of India, and foreign tourists constantly arrive at the international airport from all over the world to visit India and also to visit Delhi because of its historical monuments.

There are all kinds of hotels: five star, medium, budget class, and low-budget class. I am sure foreign tourists always stay in luxurious hotels or budget-class hotels (backpackers mostly stay here), but no one likes to stay in low-budget hotels. These low-budget hotels are for the middle-class local people who always travel with their families and would not dare to sleep at the railway platform or on the footpath. Rickshaw pullers are agents of these hotels, and they do not wait for rich tourists but always catch the middle class at the railway station or bus station and take the passengers to these particular low-budget hotels. For this job these rickshaw pullers get a tip of around ten or twenty rupees from the hotel owners. However, the car drivers get more than the poor rickshaw pullers.

Some of the car drivers who recommend the hotels to tourists get about 30 percent of the whole amount paid by the tourists to the budget hotels or other big hotels, if tourists stay in the hotels recommended by car drivers. Car drivers always wait for the kinds of tourists who are interested in big hotels or budget hotels. So when we reached Delhi, the rickshaw puller took us to a low-budget hotel. Although these hotels have similar signboards hanging out, extolling all the facilities as being like big hotels, it is only written, and nothing is found to exist by a guest when he or she stays there. Everyone knows about this, but when one cannot afford an expensive hotel, then the only alternative is to stay in these low-budget hotels. This type of hotel costs not more than two dollars for a twenty-four-hour stay. It promises all the facilities, like hot water, TV, and attached bath, but the guests never get water in the bathroom, the TV is not in a working condition, and the toilet is full of unflushed excrement. In some hotels there are common toilets for all the guests. There is always a long queue of people waiting their turn. One feels lucky if one gets a chance to enter the toilet, but the next in line soon knocks at the toilet door and requests one to hurry up, sometimes with threats.

The hotel where we stayed had a toilet in the room, and fortunately it was working, and there was water. But what disturbed us were the awful drawings on the walls of the toilet done by some dirty-minded guest. Ugly drawings of human sexual organs with dirty comments are very usual in public toilets, toilets of low-budget hotels, and in third-class railway compartments. Dirty-minded people often draw ugly pictures of human sexual parts with their ball pen. Why? I think they suffer from sexual inferiority, and perhaps they enjoy it, but they do not know that they are just insulting human beings.

In the rooms of these hotels, three or four glasses and a plastic jug can always be seen. And if you move your bed, you will find empty bottles of liquor, cigarette butts, and *beedies* (crude form of cigarette) and walls are always covered with red spat (people chew tobacco and usually spit it anywhere).

We found in our room an empty bottle of cheap-quality liquor. The room was filled with the smell of liquor, and there was a photo of a boy, his eyes covered by a red rectangle, showing his red genitalia, gone black as if burnt by acid. It disturbed me, and I quickly threw it into the corner. But these were not the reasons we left the hotel. I was sure with the money I paid I could not expect more facilities. But the boy told me that a fraudulent venereal-disease specialist came to the hotel every evening to treat sexual diseases. Many patients who suffered from a secret disease stayed here. They were infectious, and we did not want to sleep on the same infected beds where it looked like the bedsheets had not been removed for the last couple of weeks.

This was enough reason for me to leave the hotel. I did know that these hotels are centers of drunken and antisocial people, but the information I had just got about the hotel made me leave it.

There are some hotels where fraudulent, itinerant venereal-disease doctors, who claim to have degrees in many medical fields (mostly their degrees are fake or belong to other doctors), stay in the hotels on particular dates. They do not have any permanent clinics or base. They regularly change their hotels and dates but always stay in low-budget hotels. They specially claim to treat all kinds of sexual diseases. None of the patients are cured by anything they sell. Sometimes they sell sugar pills in different packaging to the patients.

In India sex education is banned, and even to talk about it is supposed to be very cheap and shameful. Young boys in India have only one topic to talk about, and that is sex. Sometimes young boys "sin" by going to infected prostitutes and get infected in their turn. So the young boys who suffer from these diseases do not dare consult doctors or family members and become victims of these doctors. These doctors show them the images of rotted organs to create an artificial atmosphere of fear and doubt and make them believe that treatment prescribed here is the only way to get rid of the dangerous disease. Big black words written in Hindi on white backgrounds of the boundary walls of government buildings with a "particular message" can be seen everywhere in the big cities of India. Cheap-quality paper glued on the walls of public bathrooms carry the same messages: "SEX CURE" Very attractive advertisements in all types of national and local newspapers can be read every day. Lots of young people readily get attracted by these advertisements and meet the fraudulent doctors in these hotels.

It reminded me of a time when I was living in a very small hostel in Jodhpur. We had a common bathroom and toilet and a kitchen in the hostel. I cooked my own food and washed my own clothes during my long stay of six years in Jodhpur. One of my hostel mates was working as an agent for a traveling VD doctor who stayed in a low-class hotel once a month and claimed to treat all the sexual diseases. My friend got ten rupees if he could arrange for a patient to see the doctor. Later one day he told me that the doctor was a fraud, that he gained the confidence of his young patients, then told them about the terrible effects of some of the common venereal diseases, and sold them very expensive (and ineffective) medicines.

When I found out that the hotel where we were staying was also a center for this type of fraudulent, itinerant VD doctor and his or her infected patients, I decided to leave it at once, although we were sure that with the money in our pockets we would not be able to afford any good hotel.

I told my wife to pack the luggage quickly. We decided to go sightseeing in Delhi with the luggage. We hired a taxi to the Red Fort. The Fort was very interesting, but carrying heavy luggage it was not possible for me to see all the details. I was tired and asked my wife to stop for lunch. We went into a small restaurant. It was time for us to stop and stare awhile.

Suddenly my wife said, "I want to go back. It's not possible to enjoy this with the limited money we have in our pockets."

I did not reply. I was looking at the restaurant owner who was busy in a heated argument with one of the customers who had just finished his lunch and was complaining at the extras added to his bill. Soon the matter became worse, and a restaurant employee pushed the customer out of the restaurant.

I was disappointed but agreed with my wife. She said, "We will work hard and come back one day with everything reserved in advance: good hotels and good trains."

"Yes, perhaps with the kids," I replied. She smiled. Our train to the hills was at midnight, but at that very time, we were traveling by bus back to Jodhpur. The next day we were in Jodhpur, the city where I had spent six years when I was studying at the university there, a familiar place for me. We stayed in Jodhpur for a week and enjoyed it.

I thought about what my grandpa had said: "Our home is the best place in the world for you to enjoy." But we never forgot our incomplete tour to the hills. And I hope one day that I will visit the hills with my wife and my kids.

First and Final Gamble

It was midnight. My friend and I had completed our work. It was the last day of our temporary job, where we had been working for the past thirty days. The restaurant owner called us and paid us five hundred rupees each. We went back to our hostel. I had now a five-hundred rupee note in my pocket, and I could feel the weight and importance of the money I had earned; for the first time in my life, I had earned money, and I realized its real value.

For thirty days we worked hard in this restaurant. Our job was to wash dishes. We never entered the restaurant. It was a big modern restaurant, looking very clean and fancy from the inside through its transparent glass. We worked in a dark, dirty room behind the walls of the restaurant from 6:00 p.m. to midnight. First we filled the big plastic tank from the underground water tank in the corner of the room and then washed dishes for more than six hours continuously. It was a popular restaurant, always busy, so we

42

never got any rest while working. My friend and I worked hard here to earn the five hundred rupees.

I was living in a small hostel run by our community while I was studying in Jodhpur. I had been here for the last six months. One morning I was getting ready for college, and I heard someone calling, "Arjun, the postman is asking for you." I came out of my room, and the postman took my signature and handed me five hundred rupees—the money I had to pay for my monthly expenses, such as lodging, books, and a ticket to see a movie once a month. I stayed in the hostel for six years, and my parents always sent me money on time.

Just the same day, a man came into the hostel and distributed some colorful pamphlets to all the students that said, "Come and enjoy the most popular fair of Jodhpur. Free facility to go to the fair. Free buses from *Jaljog Chouraha*." We lived very near to *Jaljog Chouraha*. My friend Narendra and I decided to visit the fair in the evening, as there was nothing in our life for entertainment—no television, no sports, and only a movie once a month.

It took about half an hour to reach the fair by the free bus. A big wooden gate was fixed there, decorated with artificial plastic flowers. It was very crowded, with lots of shops. Music was being played at its highest volume, a bit painful for the ears. Mostly school and college boys were wandering in groups. We reached the ice-cream shop and we bought two ice creams. It was a very hot evening.

There was a shop in the corner, very small, but crowded. Nobody could see what was going on at the shop from a distance. So we moved slowly toward the crowd. We tried to see what was going on in the shop and found a man sitting on a chair, facing a wooden table. He was surrounded by people.

An iron metal cabinet was positioned behind the man, and two of his assistants were sitting on wooden stools very close to the table. There was nothing else in this shop. At first we thought he was showing some magic tricks. He had three round cue balls used as strikers in the game of carom billiards. All three strikers were red in color, but all had big dots of different colors on one side. He was moving all three strikers with his skinny fingers; he changed the position of the strikers on the table very fast for some minutes and then stopped with all the strikers in a row, showing only the red on top.

And then one of his assistants announced, "Hello, gentlemen. You are going to see the most wonderful game you have ever seen in your lives. It is a game of luck. Who knows, you could be the luckiest person today. All these strikers have dots of different colors on one side, and that is hidden now. No one knows the secret of the strikers. One has a yellow dot, the other has a green dot, and the third has blue. If you put money on the striker that has the yellow dot, you will get back double your money. If you get the lucky green dot, you will get four times your money back. And if you put your money on the striker that has the blue dot, you will lose your money. Come and try your luck."

It was gambling for sure. No, this game was not for me.

"Drinking is bad for your health, and gambling is bad for your pocket. You lose for sure," my grandpa advised when I left for Jodhpur. I made my way from the crowd and came out of the shop.

"Arjun," my friend called to me. "Come on, *yaar* (friend, pal). Let's see. It is very interesting."

"No, I do not want to see," I replied. But humans are humans; they are supposed to make mistakes and learn lessons. The fatal game attracted me, and I was back in the shop with my friend.

Fortunately, this time I was very close to the gambler who was playing with the strikers. I concentrated myself awhile and fixed my eyes on the movements of his fingers playing so fast with the strikers. But to my surprise, what I learned from my close observation was that he always controlled a particular striker with the little finger of his right hand, and that was the striker with the blue dot, the dead striker of the game. I checked it more than five times, and yes, I was correct with my analysis. I learned the technique of this game now. I knew where the dead striker was finally placed, relative to the other two strikers. I moved away from there and asked my friend to follow me.

"I know which one the dead striker is." I disclosed the secret to my friend.

"No, it is not possible. It is a game of pure luck; even the gambler does not know where the dead striker is after he places them on the table," my friend replied, a little confused.

"No, my friend, it is not a game of luck. It is a trick, a mastery he has over these strikers after long practice," I lectured him. "But let's go," I asked him halfheartedly.

"Well, what about if we test your analysis that it is not luck. I think that you, like the great archer Arjun of the Mahabharta, will never miss the target," he encouraged me. Being flattered by being appreciated is, I think, a bad weakness of human character. I could not say no.

My friend kissed the note and handed me ten rupees. I took my position again, more serious this time, waited, concentrated, watched carefully, spotted the dead striker, and kept note of one of the other two strikers. I was sure it was the one with either the green dot or the yellow dot. The gambler revealed the hidden sides of the strikers. Yes, I judged well; it was a lucky striker with a green dot. We got fifty rupees. Wow, what a win. Our eyes sparkled, mouths wide with a great smile. We had won forty rupees within two minutes. It was not luck, for sure, but the trick I had understood. I was ready for the next game.

He started to move the strikers fast, but again I got my money doubled. Then it was our third go. He was moving the strikers fast on the table, stared at one of his assistants, and suddenly his assistants clapped loudly. Everybody looked at them. It was an attempt to break everyone's concentration, and they were successful. I failed to concentrate and could not spot the dead striker, but I did not put the money on any of the strikers. I was ready again for the next game. The assistants repeated the same trick, but I was ready now. I did not remove my eyes even for a moment from his quickly running fingers. I concentrated again and heard someone clapping, but no, not this time, you cunning men! I put the money on a winning striker, not the dead striker.

Wow, look at that! It had a yellow dot.

"Shabash, *wo mara* (well-done)," cried my friend with joy.

I was now the master of this game. We were ready again, and the gambler was looking uneasy now. He packed his strikers into a small, plastic bag and stopped with his assistants for a tea break.

My friend and I were now planning how to distribute the winnings. It was my trick with his ten-rupee note, so we distributed the money half-and-half. We went to a shop and bought two pairs of sunglasses and two leather belts. We were highly excited and very happy.

After spending an hour, we decided to go back to the hostel. But we both failed to understand the weakness of human nature, longing to get more and more. We could go to the fair's main gate directly but instead took a tour round the fair again. Both of us wanted to go back to the same shop, the shop with the fatal attraction.

We decided to play a final game there. We collected all the money we had: our winning money, my five hundred rupees my parents sent me, and three hundred rupees from my friend. I now had eleven hundred rupees in my hand. We were going to do the big deal of our life—bigger than we had ever done at the age of seventeen.

I took my position once again near the gambler's table. I watched the game. He was making the same mistake. I did not know whether it was habit, or he did it intentionally, placing the dead striker with a final touch of the little finger of his right hand.

He started to play again. I fixed my eyes; he stopped, and yes, the dead striker was on the left corner. I was about to put the money on the striker that was at the right corner. But oh my God, what a mistake I was about to make. The tall man who was next to me put a huge bundle of notes on the dead striker with a great smile on his face. For the first time in my life, I was seeing such a large amount. My hands shook, my mind jammed, my senses left me for a while, and with a "sorry," I changed the direction at the final moment and put the money on the piles of notes. I did not know why I did it, but it was a blunder. I had missed the target. The great archer, who was not supposed to miss, missed this time. Yes, I had put the money on the striker with the blue dot, the dead striker. I took a deep breath, knelt down, collapsed, and closed my eyes. Alas, I lost everything. I felt a pain in my heart like I never experienced before. I heard someone laughing loudly, opened my eyes, and saw the brightness in the eyes of the three men. I turned toward the man who had lost much more than me: no expression on his face—what a strong man he was! The gambler packed his strikers and finished his last game.

I came out of the shop followed by my friend. He put his hand on my shoulder. I wanted to cry, but no, I stopped, controlled myself, and looked at the clear sky with twinkling stars.

"I am sorry, yaar. I did not want to do this," I whispered.

"No, Arjun, it's not your mistake; forget it." What a friend he was. We walked toward the main gate. Our legs felt like lead.

Suddenly my friend cried, "Arjun, look at that bloody man!" My God, the man who had lost a big amount with me was now sitting in the chair where the gambler was sitting a while ago. So he was the great gambler who defeated us. But we could not do anything. I thought no, the great gambler did not defeat us, but I had been defeated by myself, by my greed to get more—the weakness of human nature.

All four gamblers were smiling and waved their hands to us, saying good-bye. We learned a lesson that day: you win and win if you gamble, but finally you lose, because you cannot overcome yourself.

We were the losers now; we had lost the money our parents sent to us for our studies. Yes, we robbed them; their own beloved kids had robbed them, but we would pay. We would work hard and earn their money back. It was about 9:00 p.m., and we were waiting for the owner to come out of a restaurant. We were sitting on a wooden table, and a signboard was hanging over us fixed on a wall that said Vacancy For Dishwashers.

Is She Sick?

"Why are you cooking food?" I asked my headmaster.

He did not reply. I asked again, but he did not reply.

I changed my question this time. "Is she sick?" I asked, pointing to his wife.

She was sitting in a corner of the room, reading a storybook. She was looking well, but I was worried and feeling uncomfortable here. I knew she was sick, and this could be the only reason that she would allow her husband to cook. I was not in the habit of poking my nose into another's personal matters. But here something was wrong, and I thought I should help them.

Now I got very serious and went up close to him and told him, "It's better that we think about her rather than our dinner. I ought to go to the village *Sarpanch's* home and call for a taxi." It was the only home in the village where there was a phone.

"It is better if we take her to hospital without wasting time; soon it is going to be dark, and we would be rather

50

helpless then," I pleaded. The closest medical facility, a primary health center, was twenty kilometers from there. But to my surprise, my headmaster was busy making chapaties, and his wife was busy reading a book. They were both smiling. Yes, smiling. Why? I did not know.

———◈———

It was Sunday evening, and I had been invited by my headmaster for dinner. I had been recently appointed as a primary teacher in this village. I had finished my degree in teaching from Jodhpur and was very excited to get this job. This was a small village of a hundred houses surrounded by sand dunes, about seventy kilometers from the city. Even to reach this village, one had to travel by a mud road more than ten kilometers. There was no electricity or proper water facilities. I had been here for the last couple of weeks. I stayed in the school building about a kilometer from the village. I cooked my food there, and some students were also there to help me prepare food and fetch water.

There was only one well-built house, the landlord's house, in the center of the village, surrounded by many mud houses. Most of the people who lived in the mud houses were barbers, potters, cobblers, and other lower castes. All the houses were constructed with their doors facing either east or west. There was not a single house in the whole village with a door opening to the south or north.

Mostly in this area, the landlords belonged to the Rajput community, but here in this village, the landlord was from the Brahmin community. The house of the landlord was empty now. The son of the landlord was settled in the city. He came once, when I was in the village during the elections. He was sitting on the *charpoy* (a bed with a frame of ropes or tape) in the open yard of his old home under the shadow of the only big tree in the village. All the villagers were listening to him carefully with their hands folded. Perhaps he had come here to use the influence of his ancestors to get them to vote for and support the candidate he brought with him.

Lower-caste people had their homes on the outskirts of the village. They were more interested in sending their children to school than the others. One of the educated young men from a lower-caste family was working as a teacher in the only school of the village where I had been appointed. To my surprise, he did not get the respect due to a teacher. He stood up from his chair when an ill-mannered villager from a higher caste came into the school; he gave him his chair and sat on the ground. The villager was now sitting in the chair with his legs on the table. This action of the teacher's disturbed me.

"You are a teacher, and you should feel proud of it," I said.

"Arjun, you live in the city, and you have a different way of life, but I live in this village, and I know my place in this caste-dominated society," he replied.

"But it is changing; you should protest," I argued.

He laughed. Perhaps there was a weakness in his personality or a kind of inferiority complex that would take time to get better. It was something unheard of for all of my students when they saw me taking tea at his home. I had to set an example for my students, showing that we all are equal, but I was shocked to find out that he was not very serious toward his work. It looked like he did not want the kids of the higher castes to be educated. Perhaps it was indirect revenge taken for his ancestors who had been tormented by the higher castes.

It was very boring at night; I was alone in the building about a kilometer from the village. The only good thing at night was the sweet songs of a shepherd, near the school boundary, with his sheep. The song that I always loved to hear was about a lady.

During the day I was very busy with my students. It was quite challenging to introduce the new teaching methods, like the child-centered method or enjoyable learning as opposed to the traditional methods. The students always saw the teacher with a stick. What a day it was when I first recited a rhyme in the class. All the students were enjoying it, while some of the villagers were peeping through the windows, perhaps thinking, "The teacher has gone mad: he is singing."

I was a complete change for everyone, with new thoughts and new ideas. Teachers were still using outdated methods of teaching. Stress was put on memorizing, not on understanding. Once I wrote on the blackboard: "A cow has four legs, it has two eyes, it has a nose, and it has a long tail." I told my students that we would learn to write about "my teacher" tomorrow. The next day, to my surprise, one of my students showed me his notebook.

"I have written about my teacher, sir. Please check it: 'My teacher has four legs, my teacher has two eyes, and my teacher has a tail.'"

Well, time was passing, and I was doing my best to promote primary education in the village there.

Even on Sunday it was not possible to go to the city to meet my family, as there was no bus on Saturday evening, so I usually planned to stay at the village on Sunday. Sometimes I went to the nearby village where I could catch a bus on Saturday at about 4:00 p.m. to go to the city. Always on Saturday after school, I filled a bottle of water and walked eight kilometers on foot in the afternoon heat of around 107°F.

I was going to my headmaster's home today for the first time, and I had nothing special to take as a gift. I was feeling uneasy, but the headmaster was a very kind man, and he asked me to join his family for dinner. I could not say no. My headmaster lived in the middle of a village with his wife and two daughters. He was from the Brahmin community and was a nice man.

———◈———

I was regretting my question. Perhaps my headmaster understood. He motioned for me to go outside with him. I quickly went out, followed by him. We were now outside, sitting on a charpoy under a tree. He laughed awhile. I was surprised and asked him to explain what the matter was.

He said, "You are a fool, or it would be better if I say just very innocent. You know nothing about this world. I think you wasted your time there at university, reading only books and not learning about life."

But before he said anything else, I said, "I never saw a man cooking food when his wife or mother was at home. It is different that I cook food here, as I am alone here, but your wife is sitting there in the home, and you are cooking food. I simply do not understand. I never saw my father or my grandfather cooking food if my mother or grandmother was at home, not only at my home, but also at the homes of all my relatives. It is not merely surprising but quite shocking."

"Well, you belong to the Rajput community, while I belong to another, and we have some different customs and traditions," he explained. "Do you know what the menstrual cycle is?"

"Yes," I replied. "I've read about this in books. But how is it related to this matter?" I asked.

"Well, my dear boy, a woman is not supposed to enter the kitchen if she is menstruating," he said.

I was speechless.

"The lady is not pure, and she is unclean. She is kept free from all the domestic work."

What a secret had been revealed to me! Unbelievable! I could not believe it, but I was sure my headmaster was not kidding me. I felt ashamed not knowing about it.

My headmaster went back into the house and asked me to follow, but I could not face his wife. What would she think about me? What a fool I must seem to her now! I rushed back to my school. I knew now what a silly question I had asked my headmaster.

After an hour my headmaster knocked at my door. I opened the door, and he gave me a box. He said, "I am not a good cook, but I hope you enjoy the taste."

Yes, the food was tasty and quite different from what we ate at home. Perhaps Brahmins were more concerned about nutrition, while we Kshatriya were more concerned about taste and used ingredients that were supposed to be aggressive, like garlic, onion, meat, etc. Brahmins are vegetarian, while my community is nonvegetarian.

It was five years later, and I was sitting at my friend's home in Jaisalmer city. He offered me tea, which I accepted. His wife was watching television in the same room where we were sitting. My friend stood up and went into the kitchen to prepare tea.

A quick question arose in my mind, and before I could stop myself, my friend heard me asking, "Why are you making tea? Is your wife sick?" Oh my God, the same mistake again, for a second time. She looked at me, smiled, and turned her face away, before my friend came out of the kitchen. I was out of his home, kick-started my motorbike, and rode away.

That same day I asked my wife to explain all about this tradition of ladies not being allowed to enter the kitchen.

She said, "I heard that some people say that a lady is kept free from all domestic work because she needs rest, but at the same time, there are some other stories also. In some families, a girl or a lady is not treated well if she has the menstrual cycle. She is treated as if she is unclean. She is not allowed to worship, to drink the water from the same water pot used for other family members, to share a bed, and to touch the cooking utensils."

Well, it is a matter related to tradition, quite complicated to understand for many people, but the fact is that it is so.

I hope I will not ask for the third time, "Is she sick?"

Golden Earrings

Golden rings in the ears, a thick moustache, and a colorful turban: this was the image of a perfect man in our society some years ago.

I had two golden earrings in my ears when I was studying at Jodhpur University in western Rajasthan. One day I noticed that whenever I entered the class, a group of girls always laughed at me. I asked them why. And there was a very funny reply. They told me that in South India, earrings are always worn by ladies.

"You look like a girl," a voice came from the group. Well, that was a big challenge for a boy who was thinking he was a perfect man. The girls came from South India, and they were studying here because their parents were working in Jodhpur.

After some days I came back home. I told the funny story of the earrings to my grandparents. I told them what the South Indians thought about me.

My grandfather became a little angry and said, "The man who does not wear earrings is, of course, a woman."

Well, I was a perfect man for my grandparents, having earrings. At the same time, the South Indian girls had a different idea about me.

I took a decision and removed one of the earrings when I went back to college. I told my classmates that with a ring I am a man of tradition and without an earring, I am a man for a South Indian. But the mistake I made was that I removed the wrong one.

I had no idea what mistake I had made. After some months when I was in Jaisalmer, a foreigner called me and asked me about the ring I had in one of my ears. I told him the whole story. And then I heard something that made me run away from the place. I rushed back home and removed the ring from my ear. Now, either I wear both of the rings or remove both of them.

I came to know how different cultures have different meanings for different objects.

Great Confusion

It is a cold Sunday morning. The sky is clear as usual. Some car drivers and local guides are sitting on wooden benches at a tea stall near the fort car park. A young boy is serving tea to the customers. Some late-model cars are parked properly. A young couple comes to the rooftop of the two-storied guest house near the tea stall and orders two masala teas.

An old man is standing on the top of a house close to the guest house. He is facing toward the sun and pours water from his brass urn, which he is holding in the air, pointing to the sun. He recites some mantras in Sanskrit and makes obeisance to the Sun God. He performs his religious duty almost every day; eventually the sun is always there in the open sky.

A white Volvo bus carrying foreign tourists arrives in the fort car park; all the people close by look at this splendid bus. Guides wrapped in woolen mufflers and fashionable jackets hurry toward the bus. The bus stops, and the tour guide gives some special instructions to the tourists. Like well-disciplined students, all the tourists listen to him carefully. Not a sound comes out of the high-quality, transparent bus windows. It is a secret lesson.

The bus driver gets a signal from the tour guide, and he opens the door, operated by a hydraulic system. The cleaner gets down and puts a small wooden stool under the bus doorsteps. He plays his part honestly, smiles if the tourists smile, gets serious if the tourists are serious, and says yes in reply to any words said by the tourists. The tour guide counts the tourists and directs them to follow him. The tour guide is going to the first gate, looking for a separate place near the gate to deliver his speech about the fort. Local guides offer their services to the tour guide, but he declines politely. The guides go back to the tea stall and wait for the next car or bus. The tourists follow the tour guide; they are just like living puppets: they see only what the tour guide wants to show them and listen only if the tour guide wants to make them listen. The tour guide does not want his clients to be disturbed by local guides, shopkeepers, sadhus, and beggars. He wants to reach a safe place quickly near the fort gate.

Suddenly, one of the tourists from the group points to a signboard: an iron signboard, about four feet high on two rusted iron poles fixed temporarily along the fort wall in front of a liquor shop. Some words written in red on a white background are now the only attraction for the tourists.

Everyone in the group makes their electronic weapons ready, and bang…click…click…click…Only the sounds of cameras can be heard.

"Oh dear. Oh my God. What is this? What a pity! Is this fair?" Most of the tourists are exchanging the same words with each other. Suddenly, a young girl from the group runs toward the signboard and stands behind it. She pleads with her husband to take a snap. She is very happy to have a photo taken with this interesting signboard.

All the other tourists clap and say "bravo."

Just then they hear a voice say "come on," and they quickly move off toward the fort gate. Some want to dawdle, but others are quite quick, so there is no good harmony among the tourists now. But being lost is the most challenging, so they are trying their best to strike a balance. The group of tourists is now becoming split up. Some are dawdling, wanting to take photographs and spend more time looking at objects of interest. The other part of the group is more concerned about being separated from the guide and tries to keep up with him. So when the group returns to the bus park, there are always three or four missing, and the tour guides have to find them. This can be a big problem, as in the old towns, there are no street signs, and even if the tourist asks a local, they may not understand what is being asked, or they will simply tell the tourist what they think the tourist wants to hear: "Yes, this is the correct way," even if it is not. Jaisalmeris always say yes.

The tour guide is now close to the fort gate. He holds his position, counts the tourists again, clears his throat, and starts, "This fort of Jaisalmer is famous for its prestigious history...."

Most of the tourists are listening to him carefully. Some are trying to concentrate, but the signboard flashes again and again. And the more one wants to suppress the flow of ideas, the more they come out with more pressure. Nobody asks the tour guide about that special signboard. Perhaps they are from a country where people do not make such errors, or they think anything is possible in India. Then after a quick talk from the tour guide, all the tourists disappear in the ocean of crowds but in great confusion.

"Child beer available here," is written on the signboard.

I always go to my school the same way, always look at the signboard, and smile as I walk. Being a teacher of English, I can understand what a great mistake there is on the sign. The man wanted to write "chilled beer," but he wrote "child beer." He never thought that some of the tourists would have the same interest in his erroneous piece of art as in the historical monuments.

Windmills

One morning I was sitting in one of my classrooms. A student came to me from the roadside. The boy was very excited and in a great hurry to give the news to me and all the students.

"Big fan," he cried with surprise. The students looked at him. He was pointing toward the road and crying, "big fan" again and again. We all came out of the classroom and looked toward the road, which was about half a kilometer from the school building. To our surprise there were some big trucks on the road, carrying some unusual things, very big white fans; such fans we had never seen before. We rushed to the road. The boys were very eager to touch the big giants. We were all seeing these big machines for the first time, and within half an hour, several villagers came to see them. It was like a local fair. Then, after just an hour, the trucks departed from our village.

Now all the villagers and my students had a new subject to talk about. I heard lots of interesting stories about these windmills. After some months some windmills were installed on a small hill about five kilometers from our village. I had an idea that it was for electricity. Soon it became clear that hundreds of windmills were being installed to generate electricity. There are no big factories and industries in Jaisalmer. This was the first big project in the area, and it gave a lot of employment to the local people.

It happened about seven years previously, but some of the stories I heard from my innocent students and villagers are still in my memory.

I explained in the class that these "fans" were here to generate electricity through the wind. But a student in class seven told me another story. "It is very hot here, and the government is installing these fans for cool wind." Another said, "We suffer from malaria every year, and these fans would produce a particular type of sound. And the sound keeps the mosquitoes away from us."

But the most surprising story was told by one of my girl students in class six. The girl told the class that her grandfather said, "It is not raining here because these windmills scatter the clouds, and as a result we face drought."

Although it seemed quite ridiculous, I could understand the different opinions and views of uneducated and innocent villagers. Well, finally, I took all my students to the project site, and an engineer explained the working system of the windmills to us. It was a really interesting and useful lesson for all of the students.

Family Planning

It was ten o'clock in the morning. Students playing outside the school boundary heard the familiar sound of "tan... tan...tan...." A boy was hitting a small iron rod on an iron angel hanging on the branch of a dry tree in the school campus. All the students came in, left their bags in their classrooms, and rushed behind the building into the shadow of the building for prayers. All the students were in lines now; they folded their hands and prayed. It was a primary school. A headmaster and his three assistants took the attendance register and went into the classrooms.

The headmaster went into the eighth class. He asked his students to open the social science textbook. "Well, we will read lesson seventeen today. It is about population." He asked one of the students to read the lesson. "Listen to him carefully. I will ask someone to continue reading from where he finishes."

The student read the first paragraph of the lesson out loud. The headmaster then asked the next one to keep reading, continuing from the next paragraph. All the students heard the lesson carefully read by their classmates.

"Well, now I will ask you some questions. Keep your books in your bags." He asked, "What are the main causes of population growth?" Some of the students raised their hands while others looked down. He asked a student sitting in the front row. The student replied in mixed language, half Hindi and half local dialect. But he answered the question even in broken sentences. The teacher looked quite impressed with his answer.

"Well, my next question is: What are the ways to check population?" This time he asked a boy who was sitting in the back row. The boy did not know the answer, but just to try his luck, he raised his hand. He was sure that the teacher would not ask him. But he was caught. The boy stood up and could not reply.

The teacher got angry with him. "Come here, you idiot," he roared. "Why did you not listen when the boy was reading the lesson? You are very careless. Where is your father? Call him tomorrow; I will complain to him. Now get out of here, you idiot." The boy had just turned back to leave the class, when suddenly a Bollywood ringtone rang somewhere. It was a cell phone in the headmaster's pocket.

He took the phone out and replied, "Hello, hello." But the network failed, and he could not hear anything. Within a few seconds, the phone rang again, and this time to hear clearly, he switched on the cell-phone speaker. A lady's voice sounded from the phone.

"Hello, hello. Yes, I can hear you," the headmaster replied this time.

"Congratulations on the birth of your son." The headmaster smiled, and the students laughed.

"Shut up," he cried and left the classroom. The students laughed loudly again. They knew the headmaster's family well.

Just three months previously, his family was living here near the school building. He had eight children: four daughters and four sons, and now with the latest news, he was the father of nine kids.

The boy who could not answer asked the students, "What are the ways to check the population?" and one of the students replied, "Our headmaster knows better!"

Saltless Food

In one corner of a village far from the city and surrounded in dunes, a house constructed of yellow sandstone had been newly decorated in mud and thatched in dry grass. Children were playing outside, and a horse was tied to the trunk of a small tree near the home. A local painter was painting Lord Ganesha on a front wall of the home. He had written *Narayan sung Dhapu* (Narayan weds Dhapu). Old men were smoking *beedies* outside the home in a hut temporarily made for guests. Some young boys were drinking hard liquor behind the home.

Narayan was taking a bath in the open bathroom of his home. He was the center of attraction; he was going to ride a horse today for the first time in his life. He was going to marry that evening. It was very hot, and he was sweating. He put on a coat. The coat did not fit him, and he was feeling uneasy. But he could not say no today. The ladies were singing marriage songs, and one of Narayan's friends was playing the role of makeup man. An old man wound up a colorful turban and then fixed it on Narayan's head. It was bit tight, but he fixed it on forcibly. Narayan was now uneasy in his ill-fitting coat and tight turban, but he was smiling. A big problem occurred suddenly.

Who will knot the tie? Everyone looked at one another, but no one knew this great modern art of knotting the tie. The tie travelled from one hand to another and came to rest among the old men.

"What is this?" an old man asked, quite confused, checking the soft red material with his rough hands.

"To hang you in the branch of this tree," one replied, winking.

"It looks like a tail in the neck; it is better to put it back," a voice came from the group.

"Yes." Most of the men nodded their heads.

A young girl was asked to stand at the gate to give a good omen. All the widows who were here to attend the ceremony hid themselves in the corners of the home. If a widow steps in the way of someone, it is a bad omen.

Narayan came out, accompanied by his close friends, and climbed up on the horse with their help; a cracker was fired, and the horse jumped. Narayan was about to fall, but luckily he regained control, got back in position, and smiled like a knight.

The marriage procession started from Narayan's home. It was like a well-arranged parade. Local musicians led first with their drums, harmoniums, and brass plates, which they beat with sticks. Narayan on the horse, with his young friends, was second in this procession. Middle-aged and old men were in third position, followed by women in traditional dresses. Children were free to join any of the groups. It took about an hour to reach the mud road, where a bus driver was waiting eagerly with his small bus. He had booked his bus for two marriage parties, so he was in a hurry.

He was crying, "Hurry up. I have only half an hour."

Narayan, the *beend Raja* (groom the king), took his position on the front seat; "Reserved for MLA (Member of Legislative Assembly)" was written on the back of the seat. He was as honored as a king and as powerful as an MLA today.

A selection of men got on the bus; women were not allowed to join the rest of the marriage ceremony, so they returned to the village, dragging their children. The children were crying to go with their elders.

The bus reached the village of the bride within two hours, bumping on the mud road and dusting all the men traveling in the bus from the broken windowpanes. All of them were powdered with sand. Narayan washed his face with the muddy, hot water from a used mineral-water bottle refilled at the village pond. He switched on the disco light operated by two pencil batteries in the pocket of his coat. Small, colorful bulbs were now twinkling in the darkness of the night.

It was midnight, and the calmness of the village was now disturbed with the beating of drums. Music was not now played in its genuine form because the musicians were half-asleep and half-awake. Narayan and one of his friends were allowed to enter the home of the bride. The rest of the guests were invited into a home near the bride's home. They were all served tea and given charpoys to sleep on.

They were given a warm welcome, since guests and rain are always welcomed here.

It was now late, and nobody looked interested in eating, but the young boys asked for a couple of bottles of hard liquor. "We would like to enjoy the whole night," one of them declared. A plastic can filled with hard liquor was served quickly.

Narayan was now sitting on a wooden stool covered by a piece of cloth, beautifully patched, in the open yard of the room. The priest took out his religious book from his homemade cloth bag, sat down on the mat, and asked the bride's mother, "Is everything ready?"

The bride's mother, covered fully in a traditional dress with a long veil, nodded gently.

"Well, I am going to start the marriage ceremony. Keep quiet and nobody sneeze," he warned.

Narayan's friend went out to meet Narayan's uncle who was calling him. He came back soon and whispered a message in Narayan's ear. Narayan looked a bit tense and confused. He put on a smile, but the message delivered to him was not so simple that he could hide his feelings.

The priest spread decorations all around a small bunch of holy mango sticks. He then asked a small girl to light the fire, and he started his mantras. He invited the gods to bless this bridegroom. He tied and covered the right hands of both the bride and groom with a yellow piece of cloth. This was the first time both of them felt the warm touch of each other's hand. Narayan gently pressed her hand to say the first hello. But Dhapu, covered in a heavy traditional dress, looked down at the ground without any response from her hand. The quickly burning dry kindling added warmth, and now both the bride and groom, sitting near the holy fire, lost all the thrill of that first touch. The marriage song sung by the group of ladies was a bit disturbed by a lullaby hummed by a mother for her newly born son. The priest asked them to make four rounds of the fire and asked Narayan to make seven promises....

It took about three hours to complete the ceremony. It was three o'clock in the morning. Most of the people were now asleep. Some of the young boys who had drunk were vomiting now, and a group of ladies who had been singing songs went to their beds. Narayan's friend again whispered in his ear and went into the guest house. Narayan stayed alone awhile in the open yard, and then a group of young girls pushed him into a small hut in the corner of the home and locked it from the outside. He could see his wife standing in one corner of the room in the thin light of an earthen lamp. It was too hot; he was melting, and he quickly threw his coat and turban on one side. His wife bent down to touch his feet to show respect. But Narayan pressed her in his arms. It looked as though he was in a great hurry and wanted to complete the task required of him before morning.

"I have no time to talk," he whispered. "You know what would happen if I...." He forced himself on her. She could not make any resistance, and fear and anxiety knotted her stomach. She was his wife now, and she had just promised an hour before to accept all his decisions.

It was early morning. Narayan knocked from inside the hut, and a young girl opened the door. Narayan went to the guest house and touched the feet of all his relatives. All blessed him. He shook hands with his friends. He was looking happy and relaxed. Just after that, the bride came and touched the feet of all the elders, and all blessed her, saying, "*Putrwadhu Bhav.*" (to bless to have son)

It was time to take lunch. Mats made of camel wool were spread on the mud ground of the home. Small wooden stools were put there. Guests were invited, and the young boys from the bride's side were now ready with their buckets full of nonvegetarian food and hot chapaties.

All the guests sat in small groups of five or six. Narayan was to start first, so everyone was looking eagerly toward him. He was smiling, and that was a good sign for the guests. The taste of their food had a direct connection with Narayan's smile.

"*Shabsh mere Sher*," (well-done my boy) someone whispered, and all the guests smiled. They were served food with salt. It was because of Narayan, who won the battle last night. If he had failed to make love with his wife the previous night, then all the guests would have been served saltless food....

Wild Dogs

I knocked on the door. I could hear some men talking loudly and a lady weeping. I saw a broken plastic chair and an empty bottle of hard liquor near the door. A small girl opened the door. I went in the room; six men and an old lady were sitting. Nobody looked at me. I was surprised, but I dragged a wooden stool from the corner and sat down. I could hear a man groaning. It sounded like he was gargling. I could not see him because he was in the other room.

A young man of about thirty-five sitting among the men was talking loudly; he was drunk, and he was getting angrier and angrier, abusing the old lady, using foul language, and making dirty gestures with his hands. The old lady was replying with respect, but the man showed none to her. The sobbing of a young girl could be heard from the kitchen. The middle-aged man sitting in the corner of the room was smoking a *beedi,* continually cursing both ladies. I sat there for an hour. Nobody asked me anything, although the drunken man kept staring at me. I heard everybody arguing with the old lady. She was replying to everyone with folded hands.

"I apologize on behalf of my daughter," she pleaded.

"Shut up, I will teach you and your daughter a lesson, you bitch."

The young girl cried, "I did nothing," in a weak, shattering voice from the kitchen.

"*Chup kar Harami* (shut up, you bastard)," the young man shouted at her.

"Well, we did not come here to listen to this," an old man interrupted. "We came here to compromise, so be quick and finish this drama."

"No, Uncle, first listen to me. You do not know my shameless wife. When I take a bath and come out of the bathroom and ask this Randi to give me my undershorts, she says, 'I am busy.' This *Maharani* (queen) never serves me food when I come back home at night."

"Maybe sometimes she is busy; it is her fault, I will tell her not to make any more mistakes in the future," the old lady interrupted, pleading again.

The middle-aged man sitting in the corner threw away the beedi and cried, "Let's finish it here and send your daughter with us."

"No, Papa, not in this way. You know last night when I came here and asked this *bhens* (buffalo) to send my wife with me, she shut the door on me and called the police," the young man explained to his father.

"But you came at three o'clock at night, you were drunk, you beat my daughter, you pushed me, and pulled my hair. Sorry, I was helpless, I was afraid, there was no one here to help us, and that's why I called the police," the old lady requested. "But now I again say sorry; forget everything; you are like my son. Please do not torture my daughter. I touch your feet." The lady tried to touch the feet of the man with tears in her eyes.

The young man pushed her. "No, not in this way. I will teach you a lesson. You know your daughter is my wife. I am not her wife. You and your daughter insulted me last night, and now it is my turn," the young man warned the lady.

"But I was helpless. You did not behave well," she again tried to explain.

Now I had an idea what this horrible drama was about. I tried to weave all the threads together, and now the picture was a bit clearer....

The old lady was the mother of the girl weeping bitterly in the kitchen. The man who was shouting from the other room was the old lady's husband. He was saying, "I am helpless, and I cannot move; that is why you are torturing my wife and my daughter." He was repeating the name Rama, again and again. Rama was his wife's name.

"These greedy people want this house and my property; that is why they are torturing you, Rama. Oh my God, I have no son who can fight for me," he was yelling. He was trying to talk but failed because he had been suffering from paralysis from the last six years, and he was on a bed.

The drunken man was the daughter's husband who was there with his father and his uncles. He had come last night to take his wife with him, but the girl was shivering with fear and requested her parents not to send her back to hell. She'd never had a chance to prove her innocence because she was a lady, and she wasn't supposed to speak when her husband and father-in-law were there. She was guilty, and that was the final verdict because it is what her husband was saying, and husbands were not supposed to speak falsely.

The young man's father went out. I followed him to a nearby shop where he bought a pouch of *Gutkha* (cheapest chewing tobacco).

"Who are you?" he asked me.

"I am a teacher, and my friend Mohanji asked me to come here," I replied.

"Oh, the culprit," he smiled cunningly.

"But, sir, you look gentle, and your son is abusive in your presence. Please control him." I tried to take him in my faith. I wanted him to help the old lady, and I thought the father of the drunken man could solve this matter and calm down his son, so first I should try to be friendly with him. If he thought that I was on his side, he would tell me all about this, and otherwise he could say, "Who are you to interrupt in our family matters?"

"He is depressed and disappointed; you know these rascals ruined my home."

"Who?" I asked.

"Her three daughters are married to my three sons, but you know if that old lady does not fall down on her knees and ask me to forgive her, I will send the three sisters back to her. Then she will come to know, for how will she feed them all for the whole of their lives?" he declared proudly.

"But why do you not try to settle things down? It is your family matter. Why don't you bring it in market?" I requested. ("To bring it in market" means to bring your family matters into the open. People here always try their best to settle things down in the home. It is a local saying that "walls have ears," so speak slowly and decide all the family conflicts in the home.)

"Man, you do not know anything; it is not so easy." He spit the red liquid and smiled.

"But what is the real problem?" I asked.

"Are you married?" he asked.

"Yes," I replied.

"Do you ask your mother-in-law for permission to sleep with your wife?"

I was speechless. Here was man who was my father's age talking to me on a subject that was only supposed to be discussed among friends of the same age.

"What happened?" he asked.

"Nothing, but tell me," I replied.

"You know his wife complains that her husband, who is my son, rapes her. Is that possible that a husband can rape his own wife? Is it compulsory to ask permission from your wife to sleep with her? Man, your wife is your property; you can use it as you wish. A lady is a man's leg's *Juti* (leather shoe). It is better to treat her like Juti; if you respect her and if you embrace her in your arms, she will jump and sit on your head. You know that idiot complains to her mother that she is molested, and she is forced to do unwanted sex. Well, it is my son's wish; it is his personal matter, and it is his choice. After all, he is her husband."

My God, what was the man talking about? Was he a human being, the supreme creation of God? No. Impossible. I had never met a person like this in my life. I had heard about cruel people in stories, but he was not the man for whom I could use the word cruel; I needed a new word for him.

I did not want to stay there anymore. I went back to the room, the same cramped room where I sat first, and asked the old lady, "I want to say something to you." All the men stared at me.

"Just a minute; first we settle it," she replied. I was thinking of calling the police immediately to make a report.

The man who gave the dirtiest lesson out of the home came back and sat in a chair. The father of the drunken young man was looking at me and smiling. I controlled myself—it was not my home, and it was not my personal matter, but I really wanted to help the lady and her daughter.

The old man sitting in the corner, one of the uncles of the drunken man, declared, "Is there any way to settle this matter?"

"Yes, first send my wife with me but on one condition," the drunken man gave his decision.

"You know, because of my wife and her mother, I was insulted last night, and the police threw me behind bars for ten hours. Now I want to take revenge."

"What do you want?" the old lady asked.

"Tell your daughter to come out of the kitchen and rub and clean this in the presence of you all," he said, pointing toward his shoes. He announced this with his hands flying high; he smiled and gave me a wink.

Where is He (God)? Is this man Your (God) creation? I was going to kill that bastard (drunken man), I thought.

The old lady fell down at the feet of the old man. "Please do not do this to me!" Everybody was sitting there with closed eyes; perhaps they agreed a bit with the bastard.

I could not stay there. It was hell—worse than hell. I rushed out of the home, saying to the old lady, "Call me."

I kicked my bike and pressed the accelerator to its highest limit. Within minutes, I was out of the city. I stayed at a tea shop on the highway. I felt suffocated. I sat there for hours.

"Are you well, Babuji?" a small boy asked me.

"Yes. How much?" I replied.

"Twelve. You took three cups of tea," the boy said.

"Ha, usually I do not take tea." I paid him twenty rupees. "Give me a one-biscuit packet," I told him. A dog with some small puppies was wandering near me, and I threw the biscuits to them. People call them dogs. Yes, today I could better judge between dogs and human beings, and I think I know who dogs are.

Just then a car drove up near the tea shop, and I could see a man pulling and pushing a lady in the car. I came back home and called Mohanji and told him everything.

"It is their personal matter. Let them finish."

"Why did you call me if you did not want me to interrupt?" I cried.

"I am coming tomorrow," he replied and switched off his phone. Yes, a while ago I was among the rich, wild, city dogs. I understood everything now.

Early this morning, I got a call from Mohanji who had been living away from the city. He asked me to note an address and requested me to go there fast.

"What am I to do?" I asked.

"She is in trouble," he replied.

"Who is she?" I asked.

"She is a retired teacher."

Teardrops and Rainbows

Now I do not stay on the sand dunes during the night. Neither the sweet music of the *Mangniars* (musicians) nor the traditional *Kalbelia* dance of the gypsy girls attracts me anymore. The meaningful songs of the talented musicians and the white-plastered innocent faces of the gypsy dancers do not thrill me but at the same time, pain me in my inner heart.

Of course, nights at the sand dunes are a wonderful and memorable moment for any person. The sand dunes come to life at the arrival of native and foreign tourists in the evening. Local camel riders with their decorated camels wait for the tourists and offer them camel rides. What special names they give to their beautiful camels!

"Michael Jackson," replies the camel rider if an American tourist asks the name of the camel. It is "Casanova" if an Italian asks; it is "Diana" if a British tourist asks; it is "*Sahrukh*" if an Indian tourist asks; it is "*Malika*" if a young Indian tourist asks. All the camels are male, and generally they do not have any particular name. It changes according to the tourists, but just to make the tourists happy, the uneducated camel riders are wise enough to use the trick of calling their camels a name that attracts the tourist while riding that camel. The camel ride is the unforgettable experience of a tourist's trip to this wonderland.

The sand dunes of Jaisalmer are world famous not only because of the shifting dunes but also because of the traditional cultural program there at night. Various cultural programs are organized against the backdrop of the fascinating dunes. To stay in tents and mud-thatched huts adds more romance to the journey. Decorated tents with all the modern facilities, such as can be found at a person's own home in New York or London, provide all that a visitor needs while he or she is staying. People living in the small villages some kilometers distant from the sand dunes cannot believe that these tents have their own European toilet, fridge, and air conditioning.

I went to the popular sand dunes five years ago. One of my friends who was my classmate in the college at Jodhpur came to visit the popular sand dunes with a rich contractor.

His construction business was struggling, and my friend came here to arrange a special treat for the contractor so he could get his business favor. The sand dunes always attracted me, but I was not all that curious to see them.

But the beauty of the sand dunes was more than I expected. I had arranged a camel ride and a night stay in one of the resorts. I did not go on the top of the dunes but waited for my friend and the contractor in the resort by the bank of wide, spreading sand dunes.

Some boys with modern jeans and T-shirts were working in the camp. Chairs were being arranged in a circle, earthen lamps were filled with kerosene, and a temporary tandoor (oven) was fixed in one corner, while a table was decorated with expensive bottles of wine with shining wrappers in strange shapes. All the young boys working there went into a small tent and came out within half an hour. The tent was like a magic tent that transformed all the modern boys into the traditional boys of the desert. Now they all were wearing colorful turbans, white *kurtas* (a long, loose garment like a shirt without a collar worn in India) and dhotis.

Then came the memorable moment for the entire group of tourists, who had come so far to see the sunset from the sand dunes. All eyes gazed at the horizon to see the sun setting in the far west. It was like the end of a performance of a great magician with his last and most popular event. All the tourists dispersed from the dunes; most of them moved toward the various camps near the sand dunes to experience a memorable night of dance and music under the starry sky.

I saw my friend riding a camel pulled by a small boy. The boy had on a turban and dhoti. He was looking very smart and had an attractive smile. Two ladies fully plastered in makeup were standing at the gate of the camp with a team of musicians to welcome the tourists into the camp. They garlanded each and every tourist. A band of musicians was beating drums. They were looking more active today, and later I came to know that two groups of foreign tourists were the reason of their extra happiness. There were more than fifty tourists, and most of them were foreigners.

We took our seat in one corner; a young boy served water bottles to everyone and asked for the next order: coffee, cold drinks, etc. Hot Indian masala tea was the choice of most of the tourists, while my friend and his contractor friend quickly ordered beer. It surprised me a bit. It was getting cold, but most of the foreign tourists were enjoying this, while the native tourists wrapped themselves in woolen clothes. A fire was lit in the center, and I pulled my chair close to get more warmth.

A band of local musicians came with all their traditional musical instruments and greeted the tourists. They sat on an artificial stage, not high, just six inches up on ground plastered by cow's dung and mud. It was like an old Victorian-style stage where spectators could sit around in a circle. All the musicians checked their instruments and cleared their throats to prepare for both playing and singing.

It was a moonless night, and stars were twinkling in the open sky. A row of earthen lamps decorated beautifully on the ground was competing with twinkling stars so high in the sky.

It was good to see that there was nothing like a modern orchestral event—no big columns and no loudspeakers; it all was like an old, traditional party. Musicians in their wonderful traditional dress added more charm to the party.

These musicians, called Mangniars, are local musicians who have played their sweet music in praise of the royal family and landlords for centuries. They are partly Hindu, partly Muslim, and are a great bridge between the two religions. Their traditional dress is Hindu with colorful turbans. They celebrate Deepavali like Hindus; at the same time, they have Muslim names, and they follow the Muslim system of marriage called *Nikah*. But what surprises me is that, although they are great musicians and worshipers of music for centuries, they do not like dancing. With the changing times and to meet demand, they invented a new idea: they invited gypsy girls to dance to their music, as the girls from their own community did not like to dance. Only at weddings in the Mangniar families are ladies allowed to sing while the great musicians listen to them. Even today, it is not thought good for girls to dance in public places in many of the communities here.

The musicians asked permission to present their cultural program. There was a pin-drop silence as a man played his fingers on his harmonium. How serious everybody was there. The leader of the musicians started the program with the welcome song, *"Kesariya Balam Padhoro Mahare Desh"* (You are most welcome in my country).

I had heard this song mostly on the radio, but it was quite different to see someone performing the great art; it added more charm. It was not that interesting for the foreign tourists, as the music was slow, and the words in local dialect were complicated enough to understand even for Hindi-speaking people. But to give full respect and honor to the musician, all the tourists listened to him in silence and applauded his art with loud clapping.

I clapped for the great musician and also for the foreign tourists who heard him with great interest and patience. What discipline and respect there was for local art!

Now came the dancers' turn to perform their art. Two young gypsy girls greeted their guests, dressed in black with sparkling mirrors fixed on their dresses and silver necklaces around their necks. This was quite unusual, as silver here is usually worn below the waist. I could glimpse parts of their hands through the half-sleeved dresses. That was enough to form an idea about their skin color. They were dark, but their faces had a different color from their hands: white powder and cream were plastered on their faces.

The artificial color on their faces contrasted with their sharp noses, big eyes, and thin lips. I was sure if they had not powdered their faces, they would have been more beautiful and attractive. But beauty has no definition. Maybe they were correct in their decision to make up their faces with powder and cream. It instantly reminded me of our splendid old cenotaphs made of yellow sandstone outside of the city with hovering, modern electric windmills.

A young boy of about ten took the harmonium next and played his thin fingers on the harmonium. It had magic in its music, and all were stunned by this melodious rhythm. The meaningful words and sweet music electrified a current in my body. He pointed toward the guests and started his song with a meaningful *Doha* (couplet).

The girls came into the center and danced. It was a traditional dance specially sung during the festival of *Holi* (the Hindu festival of colors). The girls were throwing colored powder in the air to make the atmosphere more colorful. The beat of drums and *khartal* (a percussion instrument of India) made most of the tourists move their bodies in time.

The young boy's performance was the special attraction of the program. He sang some very old meaningful songs along with my favorite song, "*Gorband.*"

His melodious voice brought life into the camp. He sang two lines in Spanish of *"Dale a tu cuerpo alegria, Macarena."* Practice makes man perfect—a good example. He stood up and invited the guests to dance, and to my surprise the whole group accepted his invitation and participated in the dance. It was wonderful to see foreign tourists moving their bodies to these pure, traditional songs. It was just like pouring desert pond water into a glass of red wine, resulting in a great taste. And the quick movements of the bodies of the foreign tourists was enough to prove how physically fit most of them were.

It was more than an hour into the program, and most of the guests were now drowsy from the wine and beer. But before going for dinner, they all stood up and clapped loudly in appreciation of the musicians and especially the "little wonder of the desert," the young boy who, with his terrific voice, made all of us forget the worries and miseries of life awhile. He was really a music magician. The entire group of guests tipped the music group, and some of the tourists called the boy over, asked his name, and gave him some money.

I was the last one to join the dinner; I wanted to talk to the boy who gave such a stunning performance. The musicians were now getting ready to leave the camp. I went over to them; the boy was keeping his khartal in a small cloth bag.

"What is your name?" I asked.

"Gaju," he replied. He was looking a bit tired.

"How old are you?"

"Nine or ten."

"Where did you learn this?"

"My grandpa taught me," he replied.

"Do you go to school?"

"No."

"Is there no school where you live?"

"Yes, there is, but I have no time. In the tourist season, I sing here in the camp at night, and during the day I ride a camel for the tourists."

Being a teacher in a rural village, I was well aware of the problems of boys like Gaju and the poverty of their parents that prevented their attending school. So I did not need to ask any more about his personal life.

"You know you are very talented, and your voice is so sweet," I said in appreciation.

"*Hukum*," (yes, Sir) he replied.

I took a one-hundred rupee note and gave it to him. But there was no smile on his face; he looked at me, nodded his head, and touched my feet.

"I wish you a bright future," I blessed him.

That was my first meeting with Gaju but not the last. After this, whenever I went to the sand dunes, I went to this camp to meet him. Whenever I visited them, my eyes always looked for Gaju among hundreds of camel riders at the widespread dunes.

For more than four years, I came to the sand dunes with my friends more than ten or fifteen times a year on Sundays or on holidays. And I was now one of the big fans of Gaju.

It was the twenty-fifth of December when I met Gaju for the last time. Most of the camps at the sand dunes were beautifully decorated to welcome the tourists for Christmas. This day, which had been an ordinary one for the people of Jaisalmer ten years before, was now the most special day, and it looked like people here had been celebrating this for many centuries. How interesting it is to see a community accepting the religious customs of another, different community.

I was with one of my friends who came from Delhi. It was very crowded. Thousands of tourists were here to celebrate this important festival in the heart of the desert. I asked my friend to enjoy a camel ride and directed the camel rider to bring him back after sunset to the camp I mentioned. My friend asked me to accompany him, but it was very crowded, most of the camels were booked in advance, and I really wanted someone else, who came from afar, to enjoy a camel ride in the Thar Desert.

I went to the camp and waited for my friend. Nothing had changed here in this camp in the last four years, except the colorful flags, which were replaced every year, flying high on the mud-plastered boundary walls of the camp. If someone looked at this camp from afar, it had the appearance of an international sports ground with different flags representing different countries. The only difference was that the flags flying here in the camp were plain and in different colors without any design and logo.

All the preparations were made as usual. And unfortunately, because of the fog in the evening, the sun did not set on the horizon but disappeared quickly. High, cold winds were blowing, and most of the tourists hurried back to their cars to go back to the city, while others who had booked tents departed toward the tents.

I was shivering; it was really a bone-shaking and blood-freezing cold. We are people used to high temperatures.

Even if the temperature is near 115°F, children can be seen in the open playing in the afternoon, but if the temperature is near 80°F, there is a long queue at the hospital with running noses.

I pulled my chair close to the fire and wrapped myself with a woolen blanket, but it was not enough. So then I took my muffler and wrapped my face. Most of the Indian tourists were like me, shivering with cold and wrapping themselves. It was a good sight for the foreign tourists to see a row of mummies there, some fat, some small, some thin, all moving mummies. And I smiled under the wrapped muffler when a tourist took a photo of me completely wrapped in clothes: perhaps a new creature to show his friends when he would go back!

You feel colder when you are doing nothing. So the whole staff, who was busy serving and making other arrangements, was not feeling so cold.

A group of musicians came, bowed, greeted the guests, touched the ground with their hands, kissed their instruments, looked up at the open sky for blessings, and asked permission to start the show.

The leader of the music group introduced his team in a strange language, Hindi mixed with local dialect. I was worried when I did not see Gaju there at first, but he introduced Gaju finally, although he was not on the stage, but I was sure he was going to join the music party soon.

The program started as usual, and I knew that today the musicians were going to work hard. They would sing and dance till late at night. All the musicians and dancers worked hard, but what that attracted each and every person was Gaju with his fantastic performance.

He was the center of attraction. Everybody applauded him and cried, "once more" whenever he finished his performance. The repeated exercise of singing made him exhausted, and I could see the veins of his throat turning blue. It looked like each and every vein of his neck was standing out, but there was no rest for him. His music-group leader wanted him to sing continuously. People enjoyed the show till late at night. It was one o'clock in the morning, and Gaju had been performing for six hours. I wanted him to stop, but most of the people were enjoying listening to him singing.

Relief came when it was declared that food was served, and it would get cold if not eaten soon. I was the first one to move and just like a trained person, quickly went to Gaju and gave him some money. I wished to follow the example of the tourists, as they always tipped Gaju. I could see Dollars, Euros, and Indian currency lying on Gaju's harmonium. I was satisfied and happy to see his hard work being rewarded. What he needed was money, not words like "excellent, wow, oh man." He collected the notes. My rough idea was that the value of all he had was more than ten thousand rupees.

I was happy and winked at him, whispering, "You really deserve that."

I did not go into the tent for dinner, as it was expensive for me. So I had only booked for the cultural program, but my friend went to have dinner. I asked him to come out to the gate when he had finished dinner. I was waiting for him with the car driver we had hired for our trip to the sand dunes. It was very cold, so I asked the driver if we could sit in the car. I sat in the car, and he switched off the light of the car. It was very quiet. I tried to sleep, but it was too cold. I saw someone sitting in the corner of the gate. I tried to see who it was. I got out of the car and went over. I saw a young boy sobbing there.

"Who are you?" I asked.

The boy looked at me. My God, it was Gaju, the great little musician.

"What happened?" I put my hand on his shoulder. He was shivering.

"Nothing," he replied.

"What are you doing here? Why did you not go to home? Where are your friends?" I was asking him questions without giving him time to answer.

"I am very tired," he sobbed and touched my feet with wet hands. I could feel the warmth of his tears when I took his hand in my hand and sat down next to him.

"Babuji, people should not give me tips." He was weeping.

"Why?" I was shocked. "You deserve that; you work hard. It is not begging; it is the reward for your hard work."

"But they give me only one hundred rupees daily."

"Who?" Blood came into my eyes. "Who takes your money from you?"

"Other people who perform with me. They give me the chance to perform with the group only on the condition that they would pay me one hundred rupees for the program."

"Why do you join them?"

"Then what can I do? These guests would not come to my home to listen to my music. And I cannot beg every tourist to listen to my music on the dunes there."

"Why do you not complain to your relatives and take their help?"

"My relatives...." He tried to smile but failed. "The leader of the group is my uncle. Where can I go to complain?"

"I will talk to him right now," I suggested.

"Of no use," he replied, taking a deep breath.

"Where is he?" I asked.

"He and his friends had a drink and went into the city by the jeep they always come by. They all live in the city."

"Where do you live?"

"I live in a small village five kilometers from here."

"How will you get there?"

"On foot."

"My God, where is your camel?"

"That is my uncle's camel. He does not allow me to ride the camel for my own use."

"But it is very cold. How will you go?"

"As I always go. Nothing is new for me."

"May I help you today? You can come with us, and we will drop you at your home."

"Thank you, sir, but my village is surrounded by dunes, and there is no road."

I thought to give him some money, but that would be not enough: he needed more than money.

"You know, Gaju, what is the problem with you?" I tried to console him. "You are not educated; if you are educated, nobody could dare to cheat you."

He was listening to me like a nursery-school student.

"But—"

"Yes, you can do it. You know if you can sing and dance, you can read and write as well."

He smiled.

"Seriously, singing and dancing are also part of education. Promise me that you will try to read and write. A pen is like your harmonium; it is not only an instrument to play on, but it can be used against injustice."

"I know your friends who cheat you are not true artists. An artist has a heart to feel; your friends are just copying the art, and a copy does not last long. You are a genuine artist; you sing by your heart, and that touches others. Come on."

He promised. He stood up. We shook hands.

Teardrops from his eyes were falling on sand below our feet. His teardrops were like the first drops of the monsoon after the extreme summer that evaporate quickly but lead other drops to quench the thirst of the hot land. The first drops are always sacrificed but enable the next ones to flourish. So Gaju was the first drop, who with his inner strength could win a way for the next generations of great artists to come.

"God helps those who help themselves," I said.

The cold wind was blowing fast, and I saw him disappearing into the darkness. I prayed for him to see the light of education, light that would awaken the soul of this great little artist.

My friend shook me. "What are you looking at?"

"A falling star in the sky there." I pointed toward the star with a shining tail, hurrying to the horizon.

"What happened?" he asked me when he looked at me in the light of the car.

"Nothing. These two stupid sockets always leak," and I kept my palms on my eyes.

I will always remember him; teachers always love a beautiful and lovely student as well as the other students.

I was back to my village school the next day, quite tired but busy again with students of my school. It was prayer session, and all the students were lined up with folded hands in the open ground of the school campus. As the prayer started, all the students closed their eyes and began to sing. As they completed the prayer, I told them to sit on the ground. I started to call their names to fill the attendance register: "Girdhar, Girdhar...." There was no reply. A boy who comes to school regularly was not present today. I tried to check it again; yes, he was present, but he was not listening to me. He was busy looking toward the remote dunes. I could see the glimpse of joy on his face, and his eyes were shining. To my surprise, I could see colors at the horizon; it was a rainbow. All the students now looked in the same direction, and now they were gazing toward the sky where a colorful bright rainbow had appeared. I could see so many rainbows in the eyes of those hundreds of students; all were hoping for a bright future. And I wished my little friend Gaju would also be among some students gazing at the rainbow, a light of hope.

Sleeping Boy

This is a tragic story of small boy. Better yet, I would say it is the unusual life story of a child. What happened to him usually happens at middle age, most of the time, but he suffered it at the beginning of his life, at the ages of six.

It was July, and he was back in class one again. I saw him sitting in the back row among the newcomers.

"Ramesh, how are you?" I asked.

He looked at me, did not speak, closed his eyes, and slept.

Here in the village, the age for first admission into school is about six, quite the opposite of the city. In the city parents get alarmed when their children start to speak properly, and then they run for the school admission form. At the age of four, when children should still be full of wonder in the world of toys, the city children carry heavy English and Hindi textbooks and boring arithmetic books. Most of the parents are so ambitious that they are not ready to accept that their child was not top of the class. Extra pressure on small children and on teachers to learn and teach respectively make some children act like they are born old, while nursery teachers act like inspectors rather than kind-hearted teachers.

How innocent the newcomers are in the first class, always forgetting my name, calling me by strange names, talking loudly, playing with anything they have, and making toys out of them.

Ramesh was back in the same class again. I had tried my best last year, but he had failed again. Whenever I asked him anything, he stared at me, said nothing, looked down, and was lost again in his own world, a world of sleep. He never responded in class. He was not interested even in playing with other children. What he liked was just to sleep and only sleep. He slept in class, he slept during prayers, and even during break I saw him sleeping. He looked healthy enough, but sleeping everywhere had become his habit. I thought he was sick. I talked to my fellow teachers, but no one took it seriously: "He is growing up, all will be OK."

But he was sleeping too much, and that was not normal.

"Hey, Ramesh, open your eyes. Where is your book?" I asked when the new term started.

He opened his drowsy eyes and stood up slowly, taking support from another boy's shoulder. He came to me and showed his book.

"Copy these letters in your notebook," I asked him.

He nodded, went back to his favorite place at the back row, took his pencil, and started to write. Within a few minutes, he was asleep again, using the support of the wall at his back. It was a repeat scene of last year. I wanted to help him.

"Where is your father?" I asked.

"Home." He was always in the habit of answering in a single word.

"Tell him I want to meet him," I told him.

He nodded his head as usual, without any expression on his face. It took a week for his father to report to the school.

I was annoyed. "I called you last Monday."

"Ramesh did not tell me," he replied. I was sure he was lying.

"But Ramesh told me that you said you have no time."

He stared at Ramesh. "Actually, I was busy at home."

"He and my uncles play cards the whole day," Ramesh said. Perhaps he thought playing cards was important work and was part of the daily routine of a man.

"Shut up," Ramesh's father cried.

"You have time for playing cards but not for your son," I complained.

"But what is the matter?" He seemed in a hurry; perhaps his friends were waiting for him to play cards.

"Ramesh always sleeps in class, and he has been sleeping since the day of his admission into school last year. I believe that he is sick. It would be better if you took him to see a doctor," I suggested.

I saw some lines of worry quickly appear on his thin face. "Yes, sir, I will go tomorrow," he replied.

He left, and Ramesh was again returned to his favorite place in the back row. The next day Ramesh was back in class.

"You did not go with your father?"

He said nothing.

I waited, but the fact that he came into school without any time off over the next few days meant his father was not serious about seeing the doctor. I asked Santu, his elder sister, who was reading in the fourth class.

"Tell your father to go to the doctor with Ramesh."

The girl was very smart and quickly replied, "My father says he is not sick; it is because of some evil powers that he sleeps, but he will be well soon."

Again the same problem. I am dealing with villagers and their beliefs in ghosts, spirits, and demons, etc., I thought.

"You know, Santu, your brother is not controlled by any evil powers. You should tell your mother."

"She knows," Santu replied.

I was sure that there was something wrong with Ramesh. The next day I bought some notebooks and colored pencils for Santu. "These are for you."

It was like the most precious gift she ever had in her life. The girl was now very happy. Perhaps there is no better gift than colored things for primary students.

"Does Ramesh sleep at night?" I asked.

"Yes, he sleeps the whole time but—"

"But what?"

"Sometimes when he does not sleep, he becomes sick. He cries and says that there is pain in his whole body, and then my father gives him something."

"What 'something'? Tell me."

"It is medicine, my father says, but I know that it is not medicine because my grandpa and my other uncles take it every day."

"What is that? Please tell me if you know."

"It is opium. My brother takes opium every day."

"Oh my God, little Ramesh is an addict!"

A six-year-old boy addicted to taking a drug! And who did this to him? His own parents, curse them! I was shocked. I could not believe it, but that was the truth for sure. I tried to act normal but failed. Ramesh's face was with me everywhere.

At break time I told Ramesh and Santu, "I am coming with you to your home."

The girl was a bit afraid. Perhaps she was thinking that I was going to complain to her parents, but Ramesh showed no feelings.

It took about ten minutes to reach their home on the outskirts of the village. I saw Ramesh's father and other men playing cards there. One of them suddenly stood up and rushed away, holding something like a bottle in his hand and hiding it in his shirt. They all stood up, greeted me, and quickly brought a charpoy for me.

"Sit here, sir," Ramesh's father said. "Make a cup of tea," he shouted into the house. "Add extra sugar and milk," he added.

"No thanks, I do not take tea," I replied.

"You are our guest, sir. Actually, I cannot offer you what we are drinking now, as you are a teacher," he smiled, and I was sure they were drinking liquor. The odor of hard country liquor was in the air.

"Do you think this is the time to drink?" I hesitated, because of any unwelcome reaction from them. But I could not stop myself. Well, it was not good to poke your nose into personal matters, but being a teacher, I was sure that they would not use any offensive language to me that they might use when drunk.

They were looking ashamed of what they were doing, but I was sure my words were like drops that roll down quickly without penetrating a smooth, oily, earthen waterpot.

A young boy came out with a kettle of tea and cups. He served me tea, and I took it, although usually I did not drink tea, but to reject the offer might seem discourteous.

I sipped the tea. It was too sweet, and I could feel the layers of sugar on my lips.

"You know I came here to talk about Ramesh," I said, looking at Ramesh's father.

"I know, but he is well now," Ramesh's father replied.

"No, he is not well," I replied quickly. "He sleeps the whole day, he learns nothing, he hardly speaks, and you think he is fine."

"Some boys are slow in learning," a man interrupted.

"Maybe, but this is not Ramesh. He does not have that problem. I told you to go to the doctor with him."

"I went to the doctor when he was about four years old, but there was no improvement. He suffered from regular influenza and coughs. He could not sleep at night and was coughing the whole night. The doctor gave some treatment, but there was no improvement. He advised me to go to Jodhpur, but you know I have seven children, and I cannot afford so much for their treatment," Ramesh's father pleaded cunningly.

"But you have money to buy drink?" I looked at him with hatred. "So what did you do for him?" I was feeling restless.

He hesitated awhile and spoke, "We used a domestic treatment."

"What is that?"

"You know it is not harmful; our ancestors used it."

"They did not use it when they were five years old," I rebuked him this time.

He wanted to give me a lesson on the virtues of opium, and I was not ready to hear a word from him on this matter, as Ramesh and some other children were there listening.

"Stop this nonsense!" I tried to control myself.

He was angry now. "What is there in English medicines…Opium, sir…just as it is mixed and what we use is pure…more powerful…more effective."

"Who told you?"

"You can see the results. Ramesh has no more problems, he does not cough at night, he sleeps peacefully, and he does not disturb us anymore," Ramesh's father explained.

"Yes, he does not disturb you anymore, and that suits you. He is not well. You know this very well, but you do not want to accept the reality. You are ruining his life, man; you are ruining him," I cried. "You know, people worship stones in order to have children, and you are here ruining the life of your own son. You are the worst father I have ever met in my life." I closed my eyes with hatred.

Ramesh's father looked down, worried, and perhaps, just for relief, he wanted more liquor to drink now. As many of the villagers say, "Liquor is the only medicine to get rid of all the worries," and it is the only root of all the worries.

I could hear a lady whispering behind the mud-thatched wall of Ramesh's home, and I was sure it was his mother. She wanted to talk but was not allowed to talk to strangers.

"I do not want to harm you, but if you do not go to the doctor this time, I am going to complain to the police, and I assure you that you will be punished for the crime of conspiracy to kill," I warned.

They were all stunned and shocked at my unexpected reaction.

"But he is my son, and who kills his own son?" Ramesh's father reacted.

"You...." A thin, shattered voice came from inside the home. It was Ramesh's mother. When sons are unhappy or in trouble, their mothers come first to help them. This was true now. I was confident now that I had the support of Ramesh's mother, and that was something more powerful than my threatening. Now Ramesh's mother appeared as a rescuer for Ramesh, her own son.

The next day I saw Ramesh with his parents at the bus stop waiting for the bus to the city. I could see the change in the eyes of Ramesh's mother. She was not covering her face, and she was more concerned about Ramesh's health than anything else.

About the Author

Arjun Singh Bhati acquired his MA in English literature before embarking on his writing career, and currently lives in Rajasthan, India, where he is a senior teacher in the town of Jaisalmer. In addition to writing and teaching, he hosts the US radio show, *Around the World with Arjun Singh.*

Email ID—teacherarjun@yahoo.com

Printed in the United States
By Bookmasters